Praise for Summer Devon's *Revealing Skills*

"This romantic adventure is a humorous tale of magic and mayhem. The sexual energy that sizzles between these two unlikely characters sparks magic whenever they touch. Readers will find themselves laughing at the antics of the flighty Gilrohan and gasping with pleasure at his sexual prowess. This captivating tale is quick, amusing and arousing."

~ Romantic Times

"I love, love, love Summer Devon's breezy, funny (but not wacky) writing style and some of the dialogue just made me laugh out loud. The chemistry between Gil and Tabica as well as their relationship and friendship is just so much fun to read about... I really enjoyed the obscure pop culture references that Devon cleverly weaved into the story. Good times...Do yourself a favor and definitely get this book. You won't be sorry. Go. BUY IT NOW."

~ Dionne Galace

"Revealing Skills is an exciting fantasy with a new perspective which is refreshing and intriguing. Morphlanges are an entirely new spin on the tired old shapeshifter mode, and readers of fantasy will appreciate this as well as shifter fans in general. Gilrohan and Tabica are individuals immediately appealing to the reader, and the story is populated with well-drawn secondary characters. Summer Devon has penned a winner in the fantasy sweepstakes."

~ Frost, Two Lips Reviews

Revealing Skills

Summer Devon

A SAMHAIN PUBLISHING, LTD. publication.

Samhain Publishing, Ltd.
512 Forest Lake Drive
Warner Robins, GA 31093
www.samhainpublishing.com

Revealing Skills
Copyright © 2006 by Summer Devon
Print ISBN: 1-59998-396-6
Digital ISBN: 1-59998-240-4

Editing by Jessica Bimberg
Cover by Vanessa Hawthorne

First Samhain Publishing, Ltd. electronic publication: December 2006
First Samhain Publishing, Ltd. print publication: June 2007

Dedication

To the women of Romance Unleashed. PBO and buckets and promises of future drinking binges have kept me sane for years. And many thanks to Jennifer and Laurie. May you have the benefit of a thousand sit-ups without a single aching muscle.

Thank you.

Chapter One

They could not have known Gilrohan's true identity, or at least his true nature, or they would never have allowed any creature to penetrate his cell.

Certainly not such a convenient animal as now sat eating Gil's meager portion of gruel. Full daylight didn't reach this cold, dank cell where he languished so he couldn't make out the animal's colors—though that sort of detail hardly mattered.

"So, Master Rat, have you heard why I am here? I bloody well haven't—not a word," he complained. "But doesn't matter now I have you, my friend." Stretching out his long legs, he smiled into the twilight gloom. He watched the animal lap up the last of the gruel from the battered wooden bowl. "I think we have a few days to become better acquainted before I have to start work."

The rat-like creature sitting next to him cleaned its whiskers thoroughly and scratched at its round ear. Gilrohan didn't know the species but after it had finished his dinner, it had not tried to make him dessert and that seemed friendly enough.

"Tell me about yourself..." He gazed at the creature. It had the same sort of pointed nose as his first tutor. That decided the matter. "Tell me, Master Blongette. Do you survive on prisoner's fare?"

The creature vigorously licked its belly then curled into a ball.

"I am honored that you feel you may relax in my company. But you are in the center of my slab."

He sighed and moved to the damp stone floor. Hardly worse than the rock shelf of a bed. And he did not want this rat thing to flee. It would soon be time for the flow and he'd at last be able to call upon the power he hadn't used for years. This rat would be the perfect form to slide out of the prison.

The rat trundled off but it reappeared soon after the next serving of gruel was shoved through the slot in the cell door.

Though he felt constant hunger, Gilrohan left much of the watery gray slop for the animal and when it visited over the next few days and nights, he sat near the rodent and shared his meals. Eventually he could even stroke the creature, and as he did so, gently tweak out its hairs. Ahhh, good. He gagged down the hairs and slowly, day by day, felt the returning force that would alter him.

At last he could shed his clothes and perform the final, uncomfortable transformation that only took a matter of a moment or two.

With a wiggle and an exhalation, he slipped through the bars.

On silent rat paws, he pushed under one cell door after another. None of the five men who'd accompanied him were held prisoner. He prayed that they'd been released and not slaughtered.

He had more exploring to do, but after a moment's hesitation, he scampered back into his own prison cell. With a huge effort, he dragged the unconscious rat he called Master Blongette after him—partly because he had grown fond of the animal and did not want to leave it exposed to danger, but mostly because he did not want the jailers to see the stunned form and realize his method of escape and his nature. Morphlanges were considered unholy demons in these primitive areas. Bad enough being a prisoner. He wasn't interested in torture. He even considered going back for the rags they'd given him to wear, but rejected the idea. Too much work for a creature who needed food and freedom.

He pulled the unconscious Master Blongette under a shrub in a hidden part of a garden and waited. Allowing his temporary rat nature to take over, he passed the time grooming himself. At last the unconscious creature stirred. It took one look at him, hissed with alarm and streaked off into the night.

Goodbye, my friend, he squeaked after the panicked animal.

He had a half round, perhaps thirteen days, before he'd lose his power and animal form would slide from him again. In the meantime, he could explore this stronghold. Good. He rubbed his little paws together eagerly.

His king had sent him as an honest emissary. By throwing him in prison, the baron of this manor, which was more like a castle, had given him leave to act as a dishonest spy.

Perhaps for his next transformation he'd take on a tiger and eat the damn Lord Lerae, the fool who'd put him in prison.

He didn't want to go back into the keep but he had work to do. First he would climb the stone stairs to the bedchambers and spy on the lady his king wanted for the oldest prince. She was the reason for his ill-fated journey, after all.

He couldn't be sure his king would reject the female just because her brother the baron had atrocious manners and was prone to drugging and imprisoning his guests. Gilrohan's king enjoyed a challenge. Besides, King Ronan wanted a female from an outlying northern barony. This female was the prettiest earlier scouts had found.

Before he'd come to this godforsaken keep, Gilrohan'd memorized a map and had a fair notion of where to find the young woman. He found her chamber quickly enough, and there he discovered a reason why she would not suit the king's son.

In the dim light of a single candle, she sprawled naked on the bed, her hair spread over a pillow. An angelic smile crossed her face as she watched a man undress.

Gilrohan slid silently farther into the room, trying to identify the man. Large and at least twenty years older than the slim girl on the bed, the man looked vaguely familiar. One of the lord's advisors. Goodness, did the lord know this advisor tupped his sister?

The man left his boots and silken clothes in a heap on the floor. He reached down and grabbed the girl's breasts, one in each hand.

Honestly. No style whatsoever. He might have been milking a cow the way he tugged and squeezed at her lovely tits. The man let go of her breasts and grabbed at her head to force her over to his cock.

Gilrohan squeaked his disapproval. *Crude and unimaginative.*

The girl lay on her side and sucked eagerly. She seemed pleased. Gilrohan, fascinated, scooted closer. At least she had some skill, unlike her partner who continued to maul her breasts with one hand. With the other, he patted her head as if she were a dog.

Eventually the man pushed her over and clambered onto the bed. He lowered himself between her legs and thrust into her without a single touch of his fingers to see if she was ready.

I treat paid women better than that, Gilrohan informed the rutting couple.

Yet the man's style must have been to the lady's liking, for she was soon panting, and in the dim light, Gilrohan could see her pale limbs wrap around her partner's ruddier body. His rat's sharp nose could smell her body's musky excitement.

Her pants turned to groans and as the man smashed into her harder and faster, she howled, "Yes, yes."

As the two people on the bed sweated, humped and groaned, Gilrohan thoughtfully picked his teeth with one claw. The female shrieked her pleasure and he slipped from the room. Man or rat, he often did not understand women.

Part of his mission had been concluded. The lady, enthusiastic and beautiful though she was, would not meet with his king's approval. Now Gilrohan could see about his revenge.

Before doing any more exploration, he'd hunt for food. He slipped into the blessed fresh air, stretching long-imprisoned muscles, throwing off the chill of the stone dungeon. A small stream ran through the garden between fragrant rosebushes. He looked around carefully before stepping in. Though it was dark, enough moonlight shone that any observers might spot a rat sitting in the water, thoroughly scrubbing itself.

After a good shake, he sauntered to the stables to nibble on fallen oats. And then he passed along to the hunter dogs that whimpered and howled at the confusing smell of him. Good, get them used to him as an animal so that when he grew to man again, they'd be uncertain how to track him.

As he made his way around the well-tended facilities, a delicious scent invaded his nostrils. Eggs. Oh, this must be his rat form's favorite meal, for he grew ravenous. His hunger made him lose too much natural caution and he scurried straight across the open yard to get at the sleeping hens.

A mistake.

Suddenly he was upside-down, dangling in the air. "Got you, you horrible creature."

The woman threw him in a container—a basket. "Tabica, got another fesslerat," she called across the dark yard. "Ya hungry?"

"No, thanks."

"As always, too ladylike."

A husky laugh. "Nonsense."

The hefty woman grabbed him and pulled him out by the tail again. "I'll take care of him. And maybe trade the skin for a hunk of cheese."

Gilrohan frantically scrabbled and tried to bite her, for he knew she planned to dash his brains out.

Even as the world began to rush and the wind whistled in his ears, someone screamed, "No! Don't!"

The woman clutching his tail stopped in mid-swing. "Why not?"

From his now gently swaying head-down position, his sharp rat's eyes made out the bare feet and the drab gray gown of a servant running toward them. "Give that animal to me." It was the woman with the throaty laugh.

"Tabica. What're you—"

"Please?"

She absently swung him back and forth as she considered the offer. At last she said, "Yah, if you'll do his lordship's chambers five mornings, I will."

The shapely feet shifted. The woman who'd saved him heaved a sigh. Hours seemed to pass. Gilrohan loathed both women and wished he could nip his savior into accepting the offer. *Yes. Yes, tell her yes,* he squeaked. *Please.*

At last she spoke. "Fine, all right."

"Starting in a few hours."

"Yah."

"Really? You're that fond of this rat? Sometimes you give me the willies, you do." The large woman roughly thrust him back into the basket. "You get the basket too, then. One of my favorites when I go fishing. Don't forget now. Lordship's chambers. Five days."

"Mornings only."

"Blast, I did say that, didn't I?" The large woman chuckled. "Well, his lord's not so bad at night since we started adding that concoction of yours to his wine."

All trace of light vanished as a cover was thrust over Gilrohan's basket. He sniffed cautiously. Through the stench of fish clinging to the dried twig basket, the young female human smelled wonderful. Her scent was rich, sweet and almost as delicious as eggs. He wanted to gnaw through the rough bark basket and get at her. But not to chew on her—hmm, though he wouldn't mind tasting her at that. He gave a yip of surprise at his response. *I'm some sort of rodent and yet I'm having a strong sexual response to a human. How peculiar is this? I wish Master Blongette was here to explain. Ha, the rat or the tutor.*

"Quiet, rat," she said.

I'm squeaking. That's what we rodents do. Granted, I'd grown used to talking to myself in my cell—

"I told you to shut up."

I may speak all I wish to, woman. I shall pretend not to understand you and you certainly don't understand me—

"Yes, I do."

That succeeded in shutting him up all right, but only for a second. *No. How can you? This makes no sense.*

The sound of a door opening and slamming shut again. The thump and hiss of someone tossing wood on a fire—and then the lid of the basket came off. A pinched angry face peered in at him. Dark eyes, a brush of freckles, a lush, slightly overlarge mouth and he nearly swooned with desire.

How? He gasped. *You understand me. And there's something very—*

Grimly, the woman reached for him. She grabbed him and even as she hauled him out of the basket, he began to transform.

Tabica had wrapped her hand around a thin, furry body. Before two breaths had come and gone, her hand rested on the smooth waist of a fully-grown naked man.

She'd only seen one other morphlange in her life, but even in the moonlight she had recognized this magical being the instant she spotted him dangling from Yeva hand. The shadow of his human form glowed through the fesslerat. Good God, what was such a creature doing running about the hold?

At least now she knew her mother had been right to worry. Tabica did have powers beyond recognizing the strange morphlanges. She seemed to understand them—and transform them as well. She wished the stupid human/animal had stayed away. Yet a sense of excitement mixed with her fear—like the night Yeva had stolen the guards' flask of wine. Oh, this was considerably more dangerous... Forbidden magic.

She looked up into the astonished gray eyes of the man and gasped. When she pulled her hand away, he dropped almost at once into the form of the rodent.

Who—or what—the blazes are you? the rodent squeaked indignantly.

She knelt on the floor, gingerly reached out one finger. Soon after her finger brushed his soft fur on his neck, the rat form melted into man again, leaving him panting and human on the floor of her hut.

And entirely naked.

He did not lie still for long. The morphlange human sprang up. He rocked slightly on his bare feet but he managed to clap one large hand over her mouth. The other shot out and clutched her arm tightly. His breath tickled the back of her neck as he whispered, "Do not scream."

She nodded her understanding. He slowly drew away the fingers covering her mouth, leaving her lips tingling and not just from the pressure of his grip.

She rubbed the back of her hand across her mouth. "Morphlange. I would have said something out there with Yeva if I'd wanted to trap you."

"You recognized me. I thought so. That's rare enough." His human voice was a great deal deeper and clearer than his animal. "How do you do this transformation? What the hell are you?"

"I'm chattel, sir," she said. "Belonging to his lordship." She'd automatically added the sir for this was obviously a man of high rank.

"No. No such slave could... Who were your parents?"

She shrugged. "My mother was a servant, sir." He didn't need to know her heritage. She was the only one left who knew her mother's true name and a bit of her history—and she knew precious little of that. Stay safe, her mother had warned.

"Remove your hand. I won't scamper away."

She knew what he meant. The fingers that had stirred the animal's fur now rested on a man's warm solid neck. She lifted her hand, but he still gripped her forearm. They both waited.

"As long as some part of you touches me, I'm human," he mused. "I've never heard of such a thing." He eyed her suspiciously.

"My mother was a healer for Lord Lerae's father, sir." She admitted that much just to stop those pale eyes examining her like that.

She licked her lips, far too aware of him. Large. Naked. Male. His broad, tall form told her he was no slave. The mysterious prisoner. From that exotic region called Marchosia—yet his accent was precise, not the slurred words of the peasant.

She'd heard rumors of the prisoners. They had been messengers from the king and all but one had been released. The most dominant one stayed in the dungeons. For days the mutterings had gone round that the master was a fool to imprison such a man.

Twin sensations warred in her. To get away from him and to touch him. Lean in close and taste his skin and mouth. How peculiar.

In the dim light of the fire, his grin gleamed and the shaggy brown hair and beard showed streaks of gold. He was thoroughly human now, though his white teeth reminded her of a dangerous animal still—something far more terrifying than a fesslerat. "Do I make you nervous?"

"Yes. Sir." She didn't add that curiosity began to overwhelm her nerves. An odd urge beckoned her to put her hand on his hot skin again.

Ignoring the desire, she tried to back away. He pulled her closer and she recalled his strange chattering as a fesslerat about wanting her. When she glanced down she saw that his cock stood large and sinister in the shadowy room. Just like his grace's sexual parts but slightly larger and more attractive. Fleetingly she actually wondered how it would feel under her mouth or fingers.

She swallowed hard, not frightened. Yet. "You shouldn't... I-I haven't been bred yet."

"Eh? Oh. A slave." His nose wrinkled in disgust. "Makes you sound like some sort of animal."

Her snort escaped her and she covered her mouth, not eager to make him angry.

But rather than take offense he smiled again, more kindly this time. "Yes, sounds odd coming from me. Animal."

He looked her up and down. Though she wore a thick gown, she felt as exposed as he. Judging by his gleaming eyes he seemed not to mind that he stood naked and erect next to her. Come to that, neither did she.

Someone thumped at the door and shouted, "Tabica. Know it's late but Cook wants you."

Her rat-man calmly let go of her arm and stepped away. It took longer this time, at least three breaths—slow ones at that—before the human with the sleek, muscled torso and long, strong legs shrank into the fesslerat.

"I must go," she said. "You stay here if you wish, sir. You might want to hide. Fesslerats aren't popular, though their skins are."

The creature sat up on its hind legs and cocked its head. *You should know I've escaped from his grace's prison*, it said. *You could face trouble if I am found in your company.*

She shrugged.

And I'll kill you if you betray me.

She swung a basket up from the floor. In his rat state, he did not intimidate her. She was determined not to call him sir any longer and hoped she'd remember the resolution if he regained his human shape. "Kill me? Nibble me to death with your fesslerat teeth?"

I'll find you. And I'd be touching you as I killed you. Even delivered in the animal voice, the threat chilled her. She backed away, stumbled, recovered herself by grabbing at the doorframe.

"You're safe here. I'll be back," she said, feigning indifference. "You can sleep on either bed. Yeva's being mated just now, so she's not here much."

She silently closed the wooden door behind her. What would her mother have said about this bit of magical hot water she'd landed in? Probably something like, "Run, my darling. Get away from evil influences." But she wasn't her mother. For one thing, Tabica had never been able to make her own choices. Before now.

Chapter Two

Trembling with inexplicable exhaustion, Gil crawled up onto the straw, gave a deep sniff with his sensitive rat's nose. Yes, it held her appetizing scent. He'd figure out the puzzle of the woman later. After he planned what he would do about the stupid Lord Lerae. He curled into a ball and almost at once fell asleep.

He woke when the dizzying nausea of sudden metamorphosis ripped through him. She'd sat down on the mattress and touched him. He wished she'd stop doing that although it seemed his body was growing used to the transformations, for he recovered more quickly.

When she lifted her hand from him, he grabbed her wrist before he turned back into a rodent. Just to make sure he remained human, he yanked at her. She was strong and pulled back but he soon toppled her onto the mattress and wrapped a leg over her thighs.

She twisted and pushed at him. He shifted some of his weight from her writhing form, but only slightly. Her long muslin skirt trapped under his knees pinned her to the straw mattress.

"You go ahead and make yourself comfortable," he growled. "I won't harm you but I won't allow you to leave until I understand what is going on. I warn you, I do not like mysteries." Ah, but he did like the feel of her under him.

He instinctively tightened his leg to draw her nearer. Thickly-lashed brown eyes gazed up at him not with alarm, but mirroring the desire that thrummed through his own veins. She smelled of mint and fresh-baked bread. Like paradise. For a moment, they both lay entwined, breathing hard. Lovely, full breasts rose and fell beneath the bodice of her gown. If he tugged at the loosened ties just so with his teeth, perhaps he could free them. Would she like that? Her lowering lashes and flushed cheeks suggested she'd not object.

He stretched his body over hers. She did not attempt to pull away. Instead she moved even closer and put her mouth to his shoulder, a light tentative brush of her lips on his skin.

"I believe you won't hurt me," she whispered. "Eh, but I don't understand why I'm not frightened. Perhaps because you have a wonderful human form." She drew in a long breath. "As I worked today, I thought of you and wondered about how it would feel to touch you."

After years of approaching females who slept with him only after days of hints and courtly dances—or at the very least, promises of riches—he could only stare. Her simple, direct speech struck him utterly dumb. And his senses left over from another form knew she did not lie.

The instantaneous heat flooded him, as thoroughly altering him as any of his morphlange forms. He grunted and forgot everything but the wicked desire that gripped him.

"Shall we satisfy that curiosity of yours?" He ran his hand over her body, exploring every inch he could reach. Good, but he wanted warm soft flesh touching him not that coarse clothing.

She shuddered when his hand brushed the bare skin of her calf and seemed to hold her breath as his hand traveled beneath gray skirts, up the glorious length of her thigh. Ah, blessed happiness, she did not bother with anything other than a petticoat or two under her skirts. The vision of the princess and her rutting partner came to him and at that instant, Gilrohan understood the man's eager ineptitude. Hunger made one forget one's table manners.

"No." She attempted to press her knees together but her thighs only drew his hand and arm in closer. So close, he could feel the heat rise from her body. "Sir, I must not. I am to be bred to the groom's assistant."

He stopped her words with a hungry kiss. She parted her lips under him and tilted so their mouths fit even better. Not avoiding him. Her tongue met his in a tentative exploration that soon grew bolder.

He could not resist dragging his mouth away to say, "You will kiss me, but no more?"

She gave a shrug he could feel through his whole body. He stroked the impossibly soft flesh of her inner thigh and cupped his hand over her sex. Feathery curls tickled his palm until he pressed between the folds of flesh and found her already damp and swollen.

She gnawed her full lower lip. Her dark eyes widened and stared into his. "You should not do this to me."

"No? That's not what your body says. It's telling me you want more." He expected her to try to push him away. She shifted under him and he wanted to shout with frustration. He'd never shove into an unwilling woman, though he also couldn't recall ever feeling so ravenous. The thought of entering where he was not invited both excited him and made him ashamed. He ached with wanting her. Had he ever been so wickedly hard before?

But she didn't try to push him away or protest. Instead she combed her fingers through his hair and gave a small squirm beneath him. "Yes. I want more. More. God help me, I can't seem to stop myself," she whispered. "I want you, sir."

Another simple admission that sent another ripple of heat and frustration through his body. He stroked her swelling sex and moved over the crunching straw to draw closer to her. "And what will happen to you if you do not breed with your groom's assistant first?"

Her body tensed for an instant and she closed her eyes. "What happens to your females when they do not go with the mate chosen for them, sir? Disgrace?" She didn't wait for his answer. "For me? I imagine I'd be sold or banished to the fields."

"Barbarous. We do not treat our women like animals to be bred for results."

He felt the warmth of her breath against his throat as she exhaled in disgust. "I know you came here to discuss mating the baron's sister to a prince," she said. "How is that so different?"

She certainly didn't sound like a low-ranking wretch at the moment, but his body didn't want to talk about rituals of mating—except perhaps their own. His cock demanded all talk cease.

But she apparently didn't hear its demand. "I heard a bit about you in whispers today. Your imprisonment had been kept quiet, even among the servants."

His finger drew teasing circles over her slit. "Hard to keep a secret when it escapes," he said.

"What is your name, sir?"

"I'd rather not say."

She squirmed away from his exploring hand. "You must be honest with me if you want my help."

"I don't require your help."

She tightened her lips and looked away. "Very well then, sir. Be honest with me if you wish to mate with me."

His heart sped up as if he were a foolish schoolboy and not an experienced courtier. Damn, he did not like to be manipulated even if it was not intentional. "What of your groom's assistant?"

She must not have heard the mockery in his voice for she did not take offense or grow ashamed. "He loves to mate, though I hear he doesn't think about a woman's pleasure." One side of her mouth crooked into a grin, and with light fingers, she stroked his arm and slid over the knotted muscles in his shoulders. "But I have no desire to touch him or allow him to touch me." In a low voice, she said, "I have never had a gift. You're the first I'll give myself. Lying down with you. If you tell me your name."

He spoke with no hesitation. "I'm Gilrohan." Holding her head with his hands, he claimed his reward and kept her still so he could taste her mouth, automatically tallying the amount of time he could sacrifice to pleasure. Thirteen—no, twelve—days to explore the keep and outlying structures. One day or so enjoying this woman would not hurt his pledge to his king.

"Gilrohan. Yes. Kiss me again." She closed her eyes. Her full mouth opened under his. He wanted to see her naked, to discover if her skin looked as perfect all over her. Even better he wanted to feel it touching every inch of him.

He planned to fall back into astounding kisses and eventually into her, yet, even as he touched her lips with his and sank into a deeper exploration of her mouth, the questions nagged him. This was no ordinary peasant woman. And at any rate, he had to know more about his own situation. He pulled back before his body's craving took over his mind again. "You know who I am and why I came here. Perhaps in all those whispers you overheard you learned why I was thrown in prison?"

Her fingers twined in his hair. "The servants gossip that you're being held for ransom."

He grimaced. "Your master could learn a little about the practice of holding prisoners for ransom. According to every civilized standard, one treats them well."

She smiled, tilted her head and looked at him from the corner of her eyes, playful for the first time. "I shall try to make up for the lack of hospitality my master showed you."

She nuzzled his chin, but he was not finished with his questions yet. "Who are you? And what is your job?"

"I told you. My name is Tabica. All I do is work. Sometimes clean the upper chambers. Sometimes help the cooks or in the gardens."

"Tabica," he mused. "That means some sort of strong building or another in Arabi. Or maybe simply the material? Ah, never mind. This I know—a woman with powers such as yours should never be a slave."

"What powers?" The question sounded real, almost urgent.

He chuckled, amused by the innocence of this potent woman. "Other than your power to make me go crazy with desire? I expect I mean the way you turned me human again. I did not know such a thing was possible and I've studied the Arts. If I didn't know any better, I'd say you were a descendent of some powerful practitioner but they're all registered. So? How is it you're a slave?"

She remained silent for a time as if practicing different answers for him. "I-I had never shown any sort of talent for magic before. I have only spotted one morphlange in my life. My mother is the one who told me that name for the creature—it was a wolf so I didn't go near her. I certainly didn't touch her and change her."

He rolled onto his back and pulled her body partway onto his, running his hands up and down her back, over her rounded buttocks. She kissed his throat and shoulder. And then bold as any courtesan, she reached down to wrap her hand around his rock-hard cock. Perhaps she wished to distract him from questions. If that were true, her ploy worked. Her fingers did an amazing skillful dance on him. Oh, damn his soul—she was so very wrong about not showing magical talents.

"I thought you'd never been mated." He gasped and arched up to her touch. "You know what you're doing." His body quivered, close to the edge too quickly. No, blast it...or rather, not blasting. He wanted to savor this first release with the woman.

"I haven't been, but I do chamber duty for his lordship on occasion and he demands his women servants to know this art. My mouth too. Would you like that? I shouldn't mind that for you."

Gilrohan's only answer was a strangled groan.

Tabica slipped down a body much leaner and finer than the lordship's—not that she'd ever had to touch anything more than his lordship's penis for this sort of duty. Her lord didn't require intimacy, only relief.

Gilrohan's cock was larger and she could not take it all into her mouth easily. As she licked and sucked, she felt a new, answering blossoming and tightening in her own groin. She did not have to hold back nausea and he did not shove her down or yank at her hair. She hoped he would not require her to swallow his cum or thrust himself hard into her mouth. Yet she wondered if she'd mind, for the taste and scent of this man made this familiar duty a pleasure.

He grunted and she answered with a soft hum that she knew he felt from the way he moved beneath her. She breathed his scent of fresh straw and musk—clean despite languishing in a dungeon? But she lost track of that thought as he swelled and thrust into her mouth. She knew he was close.

He ran fingers through her hair. "What do you do to me?"

She laughed without taking her mouth from him.

"Careful," he whispered hoarsely. "Oh...careful." His hands left her hair and slid down to circle her taut nipples through the fabric of her tunic. She understood he would allow her to move away from his release, but for once, she bent to this job with enthusiasm. So...delicious. And she moved her body in the rhythm of his bucking hips. She watched, ridiculously pleased she'd created the helpless, glazed expression gripping that clever face. For a long moment, he panted and she smirked—and between her legs she throbbed, excited by his pleasure.

But before the moment of his release, his hands pulled at her. He reached for her head and hauled her up for a long kiss.

"No. I will not be controlled. A gift for yourself, you said," he whispered hoarsely. "Not me. "

With one strong hand, he pressed her onto her back, and the other stroked between her legs as she lay on the straw. She closed her eyes and his thumb again caressed the place where no one else had ever touched her before. Amazing how the light, firm touch sent pleasure rolling through her body. She whimpered. *Yes. Now I want to be filled with a cock.*

"No. Not yet," he whispered. She hadn't even known she'd spoken.

"Please."

His fingers made endless tingling circles over the swollen part between her legs.

She slid her bare foot up and down his thigh, unable to keep still. Restless she broke away for a second. He gave her a panicked look and reached for her.

She threw herself at him before he transformed again. She giggled, amused by the thought of being caressed by a fesslerat.

"Not funny," he growled in her ear. "I want to remain a man. For now."

"Yes," she agreed. "Please. I want you inside me."

He cursed and gave her a savage kiss. She tasted his need and saw his unfocussed eyes, his parted lips—again the look of fierce greed. He pushed her legs apart and wedged himself between them, his cock pushed against her. Good. She moaned and lifted her hips, her cunt swollen and aching, and opened her legs wider.

But then he raised his face and studied her. His mouth pressed tight—as if he fought off the craving.

"I want you helpless as you make me." In a softer voice, he added, "We need not rush. I look forward to delectable experiences with you before I leave."

She shivered. "What do you mean?"

To her disappointment, he rolled from her body to lie next to her, but his fingers moved over her, drawing light circles on her skin, dipped between her legs again. The touch built her to a frenzy again. With his teeth, he tugged her tunic from her breasts then suckled her nipples until she writhed.

He slid down along her belly and kissed his way to the band of her petticoat, quickly undid the knot, gripped her thighs. He kissed and licked a slow path down to her quim before he plunged his face between her legs. His soft beard made the tender inside of her thighs tingle for a moment before his delicious mouth went to work.

She gave a wordless cry as the hot tongue stroked her, loosing a flood of pleasure. His skilled mouth enfolded and sucked at her clit. She needed to move and writhed hard against him, but large hands held her firmly, pressing her down to the rough cloth. A few strands of straw poked her, but anything that touched her only increased the growing heat. Something thrust high into her—his finger. So much larger and moving more boldly than her own hesitant experiments with her hands, his fingers curled into her, pressing mercilessly against another delicious and unfamiliar pleasure spot. The almost uncomfortable throb of his touch turned to pure pleasure.

The release slammed into her hard, dragging her over waves of pleasure. Her breathing steadied. Pressed to her side, he leaned on a hand, watching her.

She ran her fingers over his damp, disheveled beard. Her body hummed. She sighed and rolled her hips to savor the lingering twinges of her climax. Wonderful man, wonderful day that brought them together. And it was early yet, not even dawn.

Hunger still raged in her and she tilted her head, looking for him. He slid up her body and bent his head to put his mouth on hers. Sweet and salty with her own flavor.

She'd heard rumors of her chosen mate, the groom's assistant, and she suspected he would never wish for such extended play or even to touch her skin to skin. She had been relieved because she hadn't known she wanted this intimacy.

"You have been worth the price I paid for you," she said. "Five chamber mornings for this. I'd have taken full days in exchange for this."

"You're mistaken if you think you purchased me. You're the one who is owned, girl. I may not be the best of men, but no one has ever bought or sold me. And I always control who uses my body and how." He spoke lightly, trying to mock, but she heard hunger in him. A combination of lust with a touch of anger.

She found his rock-hard, swollen cock and gave it a squeeze and felt it harden even more at her touch. "You control your body? Then I suppose you're not interested in mine?" She started to get up—or pretended to.

Oh, but he moved quickly. He efficiently peeled off the rest of her clothes so they lay belly to belly and hip to hip. Then he lifted himself and, pressing her legs apart again, dropped between them. "I will show you how interested," he growled. He reached between their bodies and rubbed his cock over her slit. "Wet," he breathed. "Lovely. Ready."

"Yes." She wrapped her arms around him. Irresistible sensation stirred again... She squirmed with pleasure against him until, with a determined thrust of the hips, he buried his cock inside her.

Shocking, unexpected pain lanced her.

"Oh demons," she moaned. Her words seemed to inflame him. He withdrew and thrust in again. Hard. "Oh." Panic began to flow through her, but just as she would tell him to stop, get out, it hurt, the pain subsided slightly.

The pressure of him moving inside her turned smoother; though her body seemed stretched, it no longer felt beyond endurance.

He kissed her open mouth, nuzzled her hair. "Open for me, Tabica."

Wide—she opened more, spreading her legs and her whole body, for now she wanted him in deep. "Oh." A word of happy discovery this time. The ache proved to be the growing hunger concentrated around him, around that large part of him moving inside her, but she craved all of his body. She wrapped her legs tight around his waist and rocked against him as he moved and she met each push with a wiggle of her own.

So good, the heat and the nagging pressure that would explode. It ignited her. She didn't recognize her voice as she shrieked her surprised joy at the suddenly twisting warmth that spiraled up and through her.

He moved fast and harder, driving into her jangling body until her control slipped again into delicious spasms. He groaned something in a language she did not understand.

A shudder shook his body and that rush of pleasure flying out from him added to the splinters of ecstasy growing again and again, rolling through her, gathering to burst again. She clung to him, pulling him further in. He seemed to grow larger, fill every bit of her. More, she wanted it all. More. Gods it grew and touched her everywhere. Even her fingers and knees tingled and fed the pleasure. Oh more, thrust harder, deeper.

He did, and his groans increased. Yes. More surging. Harder and—

"Stop." The voice outside the circle of pleasure protested.

"No. Not yet. More! And—"

"Stop." The voice penetrated her understanding at last. "Tabica, Tabica." His large hands on her hips held her still, but his voice panted as if he'd been running hard. "You must stop. Or we might...die from this."

Under his hands, she managed to tame the shudders but could not let him go. Not yet or she'd come undone or burst.

"Yes." She shivered. Tears welled up and spilled down her cheeks. "It is wonderful. It must stop."

"That-that was most unusual," he whispered and seemed to wait for her response.

"Oh? I didn't know." She couldn't think of what he wanted her to say. Even as she recovered from the strange ecstatic fear, she had some comfort from him. They lay still, pushing tightly together, his cock buried in her, each with arms wrapped around the other. They lay so close she could feel his frantic heartbeats gradually slow in her crotch, and in his chest under her head. Surely she could never be so close to another human as this.

Finally, he withdrew from her body and fell back onto the mattress, keeping one hand on her thigh. His skin gleamed with sweat. His chest rose and fell with hard breaths as he studied her with narrowed eyes. Buzzing with exhaustion and the strange unfamiliar twinges at the core of her body, she closed her eyes.

His amazed voice barely pierced her consciousness. "You are beyond my comprehension, woman. What in the name of Sallos are you?"

A horse's hooves clopping past startled her. A rooster announced the rising sun.

"No, oh no. Time to prepare for morning duty." She groaned. She rolled onto the floor, every muscle aching, and climbed to her feet.

"My change is taking longer," he said as his body slowly shrank.

"Yes. Are you losing power?"

"No, it is you. Somehow you've shifted my abilities. Demons, whatever can you be?" The fesslerat shook itself. *Bah. Thirteen more days. I will be glad to shed this creature. I much prefer something...impressive.*

Far off, the bell rang to summon the outlying house servants. "Sleep," she told the rat.

You are mistaken if you think that I can rest with you running about the place.

She wondered what he meant, but said, "I have run about this place for almost twenty years, Mr. Rat. Rest. I will return when I can."

She pulled on her petticoats and dress, tied it in place and rushed out the door.

Yeva, yawning, emerged from the blacksmith's hut. "Morning, Tabi. Thanks for taking chamber duty." She swooped down and grabbed something. "Is this the pet I found for you?"

Damn, that woman is fast, squeaked the animal dangling from her hand. *But I beg of you to give me some credit. It never occurred to me that anyone else would be about this early in the morning.*

Tabica groaned. Why was he following her? "Yes, that is mine."

Mm, yours, am I? Did you mark me just now on that straw pallet? I should like to try again. This time, naked, and in a proper bed. We must find out who you really are, woman.

"Shut up, rat."

Yeva laughed. "It's just squeaking. Noisy little thing, isn't it?"

"You have no idea." She shifted her feet as the warm fluid of his release slid down, coating her inner thighs. Reminding her—as if she could forget.

Her friend held the rat to her bosom and stroked it. "But his fur is so soft." She giggled. The rat settled on her formidable bosom and gave a little shriek as he burrowed under the front of her gown. "That feels so nice on my skin. Look at the tame little fellow. What a sweet pet."

His voice came to her muffled by twin mounds of flesh. *Ah, this woman has such amazing features. Her breasts are like delicious pillows. Do you think she'd mind if I nipped her nipples? They are quite large and appetizing. I would so like to nibble on them.*

"Stop it," she said

Are you jealous? No need, I assure you. I'd much rather bury my, er, tame, furry little body in yours. My soft pelt stroking between your legs, hmmm? Such a shame I can't remain in morph when we touch. I'd—

"Shut up."

Yeva looked at her, puzzled. "I'm not saying anything."

Tabica rubbed her tingling skin. If Gilrohan wanted to enjoy himself as a perverted little animal, she had nothing to say about it. "Sorry. I have to be going."

"I gave the lord plenty of powders so he'll wake up late, I imagine."

Tabica looked down at her dusty feet and gestured at the well. "Do you think I have enough time to clean up?"

"Yes, good idea. He hates dirt. You look as if you haven't slept a wink."

"I haven't. Cook needed me and then that stupid fesslerat kept me up the rest of the night."

A laughing rat was an odd sound.

She walked to the well and cleaned herself off best she could. She splashed her hands and face. The cold water rinsed the blurriness from her brain. She pulled a ribbon from her gown's pocket and tied back her hair into a braid. His lordship did not like tickling hair on his servants.

Yeva stroked the rat and giggled. "Thank you, Tabi. Do you know that the Banger's out to find you? He knows you're due for him."

She groaned. "I hear he can be as bad as his lordship."

"No one is. But I must say that other than his usual love of punishment, my lord's been more amenable lately. Although who knows what he'll be like this morning, what with the prisoner still missing. I hear he expected a great huge sum for that one." She chuckled. "Oh goodness. Yes, I'll put you down, you silly rat. My, he knows who his mistress is."

Mm, yes, I suppose you might call her that. The rat purred.

38

Tabica made her way up the outside stone staircase that led to his lordship's sleeping chamber. She was not a daily house servant, after all.

Who is Banger? Your groom's assistant?

"He's not mine."

Ah, so he is the one who is supposed get a child on you.

She shivered at the thought.

Are you afraid of him?

"No, he's not a cruel man."

What a fine recommendation for any lover.

Ignoring the rat, she hurried toward the lordship's bedchamber. His lordship's snores echoed through the room. Odd, for he was usually a quiet sleeper. She built up the fire, glancing around as she shoved in the wood, but he slept through her work. The pot for his morning water stood ready. She swung it over the fire and settled to wait.

Tabica dozed a little and woke to the sound of rustling. The rat had climbed onto the large desk in the corner and was pawing through papers.

"No," she whispered. "He's a light sleeper. Stop."

Apparently not such a light sleeper today, the rat responded absently. It nosed through some of the papers. *This man keeps his records in a terrible mess.*

"What are you doing?"

He didn't bother to respond. She got up and went to stare over his shoulder. Her mother had secretly taught her to read and she could sound out many words.

One word caught her eye. "Wedding? He's going to marry off the mistress? Is that your king's name?"

The rat whirled around. *I knew you were no mere slave. What are you?*

"I told you. My mother was a healer."

A slave that can read? You are not—

She leaned close to whisper. "My mother was a free woman who was, um, captured by his lordship's father. Get going, he's waking up."

To answer your question, no, it's not my king's name and it's dated before my arrival. Your master thinks he is crafty. He is merely stupid. Yes, now he is waking up.

The rat bounded from the table and darted under the bed before she even noticed he'd moved.

From the bed came the deep growl. "Which are you?"

She curtsied. "Tabica."

"I want the one with the big breasts."

"She is not available, my lord."

"Oh very well." He pushed back the covers and stood naked, scratching at his scrotum. Though stockier than Gilrohan, he was not a fat man. His thick black brows gathered as he frowned at her. "Sponge me today. No full bath."

She'd have to clean and towel him dry quickly before he complained of the cold.

He settled in his massive oaken chair by the crackling fire, his eyes closed. She quickly wrung out the cloth in the warm water and got to work, trying not to touch him with her hands. He liked only the cloth to touch his limbs.

His lordship was not an ugly man. A regular schedule of hunting kept him trim, and he preferred to be clean. Perhaps the morning duty would be less onerous if he had a calmer disposition.

She kept an eye on his staff. Any sign of hardening and he expected special attention there. He grew angry if he had to ask. Of course he also grew angry if a servant knelt and reached for him if he was not interested.

This morning he leaned back in the chair and dozed. They must have given him a strong dose of sleeping powders, she reflected as she rinsed and dried his muscular arms and belly.

The rat wandered over and sniffed. *The man's been given a tranquilizer.*

"How do you know?" she whispered.

I can smell its bitterness. This is a despicable morph, but it has some advantages, including a keen nose. That one of your potions? It reeks. It would never pass in a more sophisticated court.

The rat went under the bed. He squeaked with triumph. *Aha, here are the papers I want.*

"Hush." She grew so distracted, listening to Gilrohan, she dripped water on her master. He woke at last and without a word grabbed at her braid and yanked at her.

She saw his cock had risen and she leaned forward but he barked. "No. Stand."

Blast. He didn't want her to do a quick service with her mouth. She climbed awkwardly to her feet, for he still sat and clutched her hair.

"My mind is too hazy. Which are you again?" he demanded. His dark, deep-set eyes seemed to struggle to focus on her face.

"Tabica, my lord."

"I remember—the witch's daughter. You're a witch yourself, hmm?"

She didn't answer. He wrenched her braid.

"No, my lord."

He pulled harder. She could feel the skin on her face tighten and some of her hairs part from her skull. Her head tilted at an odd angle because of his grip, she forced herself to hold still. Any movement might be seen as disobedient struggling.

She waited, hoping he was not in the mood for humiliation. Bad enough on normal days, but with Gilrohan watching...

He merely yawned and rubbed at his nose with the hand not wrapped around her hair. "Have you seen a stranger? Taller than me, light brown hair, scar on his inner thigh. He's an escaped prisoner. Very dangerous."

She blinked and wondered how she could have missed the scar. "No, my lord."

He yawned once more and stretched out his legs. "Well then." He hauled her face down to his thighs. "You don't have those breasts but you'll do."

She opened her mouth and got to work. His lordship grunted his approval. He kept a hand on the back of her neck to control her movements. Up and down. Her mouth began to ache, for he would not allow rest.

From under the bed came a small disgusted squeak. *So that's how you gain your expertise.*

She could not answer.

In a more neutral tone, Gilrohan went on. *I wonder why he only wants your mouth. I suppose it's simply because he doesn't care to have half-breeds littering the place and fighting over his pickings when he goes? Does he ever dive into your lovely round ass then?*

She wished she could pull off and tell the rat to go to hell. She grew so distracted thinking of what she wanted to tell Gilrohan, the lordship pushed her down hard when she wasn't ready and she gagged slightly. He arched up, pressing his erection as far in as he could, to punish her for the noise. Relax the throat, she thought. Relax. He pushed her head down roughly again. Her nose banged against his leg.

"You are a clumsy one," he scolded. "And you don't use your tongue enough."

She knew he would soon be angry that she didn't answer, and angrier still if she pulled off to speak. Yeva was probably right. His lordship simply enjoyed marrying anger and his cock's pleasure. She made a conciliatory sound in her throat.

He pulled up on her hair, then shoved her down again. "Haven't we had these lessons before?" he panted. He pinched her neck. Her squeal of pain was unintentional.

"Oh, yah. That felt good." He inflicted hard pinches with his fingernails on her neck and reached around for her breast. She wished she could just bite down. Instead she tried to imitate the squeal she'd given at first.

Something under the bed rustled. From the corner of her eye, she saw the rat saunter out from under the bed. It stood close to the lord's chair, peering up at her with bright interested eyes. *I knew he was a poor host, but I had no idea he was such an unpleasant little demon. You look most uncomfortable, bent over in such a silly position, oh, and your exquisite neck is bleeding. He does not treat his possessions with any respect. Ah, he appears to be working his nasty way to your lovely breasts. Shall I nip his nuts for you? I should, for they hang low.*

The squeaking was extremely loud, as if the rat wanted to be noticed.

Lord Lerae let go of her hair and stopped pinching. "What the blazes? Do you see that creature? This place is infested with rodents."

She did not dare raise her head or release him.

He jerked hard at her hair, pulling her off with a pop. "That rat is just standing there, staring at me. You go grab it. It must be sick or something. Get rid of it."

Wiping her arm over her numbed mouth, she straightened her garments briefly before putting on a show of sneaking up on the rat.

Heavens save me, Gilrohan drawled—who knew a rat could drawl? He scampered ahead of her and slid under the door. She looked back. Her master was yanking on trousers awkwardly, unused to dressing himself.

He waved an impatient hand. "Yes, go on. I don't want disease spreading."

"Shall I return after I catch it, my lord?"

He stopped fumbling with the ties of his over-shirt. "No, no. Go on. Get out of here. Send in someone else after you dispatch that creature."

She pushed open the door and found Gilrohan waiting, cleaning his thick grey fur. He stayed in the shadows as they made their way down the empty hall. Smells of baking bread, the low voices of maids attending other rooms, all the signs of a waking household. She let loose a breath she hadn't known she was holding.

"I suppose I should thank you."

You suppose? You enjoyed performing that duty? You're good at it, after all. I can attest to that.

She shuddered and squeezed her arms tight around herself, holding back a wave of rage. "I hate it," she managed to whisper.

You didn't seem to hate it with me.

She wondered if she actually heard a note of uncertainty in the little animal who'd been a big sophisticated man. The thought made the impotent anger fly. She smiled. "No, I enjoyed you."

No doubt about it. The rat's scurry down the long hall slowed to a strut.

You'll have to tell that big-breasted female to remain quiet about your pet, Gilrohan pointed out.

She nodded. "Now I'll go to my work—maybe find a fesslerat in the garden as a substitute."

After I have a word with you, I will return to my creeping about.

"Must you? You might get caught."

No, I don't think I'll choose that option—it might prove uncomfortable. I found what I needed in his bedchamber and will return once he leaves it.

"What have you found?"

The most interesting papers must be the evidence his lordship's sister is already married, so he never had any intention of doing more than holding me for ransom. And there is also a list of others he's held. My personal favorite is an assessment of the keep pointing out its weaknesses. That will come in quite handy.

"For what?"

He didn't answer. Instead he scurried up the stairs into the servants' quarters, pausing to wait for her. He laid an ear to a door.

Wait, he ordered and then squeezed under the door.

A moment later he returned. Before she could demand he explain his plans, he'd rubbed his luxurious fur against her bare ankle and, several moments later, turned into a tall naked man again.

Breathing hard from the change, he grabbed her wrist and pushed open the door. "Come in, my dear."

Chapter Three

The room Gilrohan yanked her into was smaller than his lordship's but larger than the space Tabica shared with Yeva. The furniture consisted of a bed, a clothes press and a desk. She guessed it was a lower servant's room, for she had never had to clean it. Gilrohan kept his firm, warm hand wrapped around her wrist as he went to the clothing press and flung it open. She tried to pull away from his grip. He paused to give her a humorless smile. "No need to be so anxious. Unlike your precious lord, I won't hurt you. Unless you give me good cause—or you ask me to during love play. I can tie a fine knot if you care for such skills."

She did not want to imagine how he learned such skills and remained silent.

He went back to work, holding onto her with one hand and pulling out clothes with the other. He held up garments and squinted at them. "Good. This is a mix of men and women's garments. I should find something that will do."

After rummaging for a time, he straightened and looked at her. "This would go faster if you'd put your hands on me, so I could use both of mine to work." He slid her hand onto his waist. "Just hold me there. This shouldn't take long."

"Oh, all right." She did owe him a favor after all. She ignored her reaction to his smooth, hard side. So warm and strong, the muscles shifting beneath her fingers as he worked. She loved the feel of him, the gift she'd given herself of pure pleasure. He'd give her more, too— information. He did not seem to mind speaking of the rest of the world. Her mother's city.

He squatted and she sank down with him and soon leaned against his broad back. Constant work and little rest meant she was usually tired. On top of that she'd gotten no sleep last night... She'd just close her eyes a few minutes.

The pressure of Tabica's weight increased. He grinned but the grin faded as soft, steady breathing told him she dozed. Amazing. How could she ignore the hunger that lit into them when they touched? He knew she wanted him. One of his previous morphs, as a junglecat, had left him with the wisp of the ability to sense extremely strong female desire while in any of his forms. Handy sort of ability in a court. His friends in search of lovers sought him for advice and he never had a lack of bed partners.

Ah well. What mattered most about this female was that her master's careless words were correct. She was truly a witch, the name the ignorant in these parts gave any woman skilled in the Arts. He paused, bemused by the thought she could perhaps even have an ancestor with high blood. Her mother had been a healer, she'd said.

He'd find the library—certainly even this primitive place had a library or at least a few Medicaments—and see if it contained any volumes on which practitioners affected morphlanges. But first he'd have to find some clothes that would keep the ladies from shrieking and fainting at the sight of his naked body. He'd be damned if he'd stay a rat any longer than he had to. With Tabica around, he might not have to.

This female might think she was going to wash the chickens or plow the hearth or whatever slaves got up to during their daily chores, but he had more important work for her.

She likely had skills more rare than a morphlange. How did she manage to survive in this backwater? And as a slave, too.

Despite calling her a witch, the lord obviously didn't believe she had skills. If he did, she'd be installed in her own grand establishment. More likely in this ignorant corner of nowhere she'd be a pile of ashes. Gilrohan would have to take her with him when he left for Marchosia. Not an unpleasant proposition at all. Something to occupy the nights on the road.

She must have fallen into deeper sleep for she started to slip sideways. He grabbed her shoulder as she fell.

"No!" Half-awake, she growled and wrenched away. A sharp tingling pain jolted up his arm from the fingers that had touched her.

He yelped a curse and let go of her.

She gasped and sat upright. "Oh, I'm sorry. What did I do?"

He winced and rubbed at his hand. "I feel as if I've been hit with a small dagger."

They both stared down at his hand. Nothing marred his skin—including fur. And she no longer touched him.

"Bedamn me," he muttered and narrowed his eyes at her. Impossible, but... "Could you actually be related to a high family? I wonder what it takes for that. Ereshkigal blood?"

A tangle of dark hair framed her pale, worried face. "What's that? Oh, no. Why aren't you a rat?"

"You've done something to me."

"I told you, I have no powers."

"Perhaps you had none but apparently you do now. Ahh!" One of Master Blongette's early lessons came to him. "After you left childhood, perhaps you've simply never met another practitioner of the Arts. I grew up surrounded by them, but you, out here in the back of nowhere—"

"I don't know why you say that about this place."

He gave her a long, hard look. She blushed a charming pink. "Yes, all right. Go on," she muttered.

"Anyway, children in the more civilized parts of the world are identified as potential practitioners, trained in the Arts and constantly exposed to others so that they will catch fire."

"*What?* How is that civilized?"

"No, they don't actually go up in flames. A near-grown practitioner is like a candle, and others skilled at the Arts must pass their flame to him before he, too, will be able to wield power. No need for more exposure than sharing a room or breathing the same air. I thought it all sounded rather like catching a fever. One tends to grow ill after being exposed to illness." He eyed her nervously, remembering some of the early symptoms of skills were very much like a fever. Constant throbbing heat that cried for release. This might explain a lot.

"Huh." She considered the idea. "My mother never said any of this. She hoped I would not be a part of..."

Her voice trailed off and her open face had changed into an expression of stony indifference. The same look she'd worn as she'd serviced her master—the look that had drawn him out from under the bed to stop the idiot.

Her brows gathered as she frowned at her knees. *Do not follow me to this place*, this new look told him. Gil might not be a genius—after all, he'd been outsmarted by a greedy, lazy baron—but he usually read people well enough.

He cleared his throat, uninterested in the surge of pity that came over him. "But now I am trapped in my true form. This is most inconvenient. I wonder if I can manage another creature before the ebbing." A sudden horrible thought made him groan. "Damn and blast me, I hope you haven't taken away my only useful skill."

No point in repining. He'd put on the garments he found and maybe convince this woman to help him cut his overlong hair and beard. Not exactly a disguise but he could find a useful dog or cat. No more rats. A few hairs from a decent animal and prayers that he could still morph.

"If I have, I'd call it bad repayment." She sighed.

"For what?" He held up the trousers and squinted at them. The sagging grey things were an odd shape and, like Lord Lerae he was not used to dressing himself.

She reached for the trousers and shirt. "In my master's chamber. You helped me. "

"Yes, but pray do not think I am here to help you. Quite the contrary."

"I'm here to help you escape, you mean?"

He smiled, pleased by her ready understanding.

She shook the tunic and held it open so he could slip his arms in. "I'll consider helping you, Gilrohan. But I want some things in return."

His back to her, he dragged on the shirt. "What do you have in mind?"

For a moment, she leaned her cheek on his back. "Pleasure."

His groin tightened with anticipation at that idea. He turned to face her. "That can be arranged. Anything else?"

She gently pushed his hands away from the ties. "Wait. Let me help." She moved closer to tie the complex series of knots for a servant's garb. As she worked, she continued her list. "You're educated. You know more about my, um, skill than I do. You must tell me everything you know about the Arts. And about whatever it was you said I could be related. Erisable."

He held his arms out so she could reach the ties inside the tunic. Hard to remain as unmoving as a fencing practice manikin when her arms wrapped around his body. He closed his eyes and tried to pretend his valet leaned close to him.

Her soft fingers brushed the skin on his ribcage.

He licked his lips and tried another tactic. A lecture. "Ereshkigal. Inaccurate name, actually—the original was some goddess or another. Anyway, you can't share their blood. There are very few in the world and all of them and their families are in the highest of the privileged classes. You're probably something far less powerful—yet you clearly have powers that range beyond your own skin."

She paused and looked into his face. "Hey?"

"I can change myself, I can do a bit of work with things I touch, but once they're away from me. Poof. That's it. You seem to have more serious skills and they must be inherited. The trouble is, I can't see the edge of 'em. I mean I can't tell if they're minor or earthshaking."

"How will I find out about my own skills?"

"By going to an expert. And that's not me. But see? I obviously agree to educate you to the best of my ability for you've already had your first lecture. "

He watched her try to battle the gleam that rose to her eyes as she casually nodded then said, "Right. Another condition. I want to leave with you, too."

He'd actually considered that idea—until she'd shown another blast of strange and strong skill. "No."

"Why not?"

"I said it already. I don't know what you are."

Expertly holding the trousers, she dropped to a crouch. "You want me on your side, don't you?"

"Fine. We'll discuss your future," he growled.

"Good. And I'll add more conditions to helping you later."

He raised an eyebrow. "You are not much of a negotiator if you think I'd accept an agreement such as that."

Shrugging, she began to turn away. "Then I'll be off to tend my work."

He put his hand on her shoulder. "Not so fast, young Tabica. I believe you are at least as hot to find out about your power as you are to fuck me."

He'd hoped she'd be thrown by his crude language, but she only smiled. "But you want to survive. That's a strong desire, don't you think? You seem to think you need my help to escape this place."

Outside the room, footsteps sounded on the stone hallway.

He lowered his voice and spoke quickly. "Fine. I agree to other stipulations within reason. And you're a fool if you think I'm going to bother with hammering this contract of ours out now. We have work to do."

She still knelt, so her face was at his groin. No longer grim, she tilted her head and studied his cock only a few handbreadths from her. It twitched hopefully in response to her close examination.

"Stupid creatures, cocks," he said apologetically.

"Mmm? I like yours." She slowly leaned forward and gave it a light kiss.

He sucked in a sharp breath and stepped to the side. "Do you know of any nondescript dogs hereabouts? One of those might serve—"

She scooted toward him, kissed him again and gave his rising cock another hot damp lick. Perhaps she only began this to prove how enjoyable she could make his travels home, but he could catch the smallest whiff of her own growing arousal.

"Stop that." He couldn't seem to move, so he tried, "You just had that mouth on your idiot master."

Instead of growing insulted, she slowly ran a finger along the length of him. Oh...growing, indeed. She nodded. "Yes, and yours is far more to my taste."

His treacherous organ now gave her a full hard salute. *Now!* it shouted at the girl. *Let me in. Give yourself to me.* Something more necessary than simple sexual desire seized him. That rolling pleasure that sucked him in and nearly killed him. But maybe not death. Just pure bliss.

She again lightly stroked his penis, which twitched, delighted by her smallest attention.

He groaned and closed his eyes. Her hands traveled up his thighs, rubbed over his belly, lightly caressed his penis. A rustle of cloth—and she stood and pressed herself against him, belly to belly. She drew his face down to hers for a long lazy kiss that almost at once evolved into something more potent.

He fought the dizzying surge of lust. Breaking off the kiss, he managed to hide his befuddlement at their contact—except for the stupidly eager erection.

She drew back, a stunned look on her flushed face. "Please," she whispered. "More kisses."

He gave an impatient exhalation. "Wait. Let's get this straight—I'm the heedless one."

She moved so the head of his penis just brushed her. "I'm usually a cautious woman, but, oh, you-your body. Just the sight of it makes me reckless."

"Ah. Oh." Her straightforwardness had its usual effect of throwing him off center. He had a sneaking suspicion that no matter which of the Arts she possessed, the one that would do him in would be her ability to spark instant craving for her every time she bluntly admitted her appetite for him.

It didn't help matters that her desire produced a scent as heady as any houri's incense, designed to make a man forget himself.

She rubbed against him like a cat, even purring at the gasp that escaped him. When he had time, he would enjoy her pleasure, that first stipulation of hers. But he fully intended to be the one in charge of those encounters. He'd dole out her pleasure and take his. It might be the only time he could control a woman with this much skill, even one with no training.

He shuddered—not just because her warm hands reached beneath his tunic and stroked over his back and buttocks as she planted small moist kisses over his chest and shoulders. The implications hit him. If she had any high blood, and he agreed to travel with her, he might be traipsing around the countryside with something as powerful as a thunderstorm but with less control.

In her presence he had little control over himself, for that matter. As if to demonstrate, his gaze almost helplessly fixed on the bed that lay in the middle of the room. No covers on the mattress but ah, well.

He captured her mouth with his and enjoyed several long succulent kisses. The way she breathed hard and wiggled against him, he knew she would allow him to back her onto that bed. Damn him, the risk that her power would burn them ought to have slowed him, yet he reached to untie the loose bodice.

His body, that should really have known better, craved more and more of her.

The owner of the room might return some time soon but Gilrohan could care less if the baron himself discovered him bare-assed and pumping into Tabica, as long as she'd let him in. Apparently she would. Phegor be praised, she groaned against him. He rubbed his groin to the rough cloth covering hers, echoing her squirms. He hauled at her gown, digging down to his prize.

The bell tolled and her groan turned to a sigh.

She spoke between kisses. "They will come look for me soon. I am sure his lordship has managed to dress himself and he will want to know about the diseased animal."

"Right. No, I don't need your help." He pulled away before he lost track of himself again, found the loose fitting trousers and over shirt she'd dropped to the floor. Awkwardly he yanked on the rest of his clothes and tied and knotted them. He ignored her amused audience.

When he was finished, he pulled on the rough knit vest he'd found. It at least hid his raging erection. "I look like a servant, hmmm? Shall I shave?"

She frowned. "The men servants are all bearded. Didn't you notice?"

"No."

The look she gave him might have been scorn, so he said, "When I arrived, I was too intent on your master and his sister to pay attention to the servants."

"You weren't intent enough. Maybe, if you'd watched the servants, you wouldn't have been drugged."

With each passing minute, she was less servile herself, but before he could form a proper retort, she went on, "Your shoulders are too proud for a servant's. Slump a bit."

He did and allowed his mouth to fall open slightly.

She walked around him, tweaking a bit of cloth here, running fingers over his rear end there. "Even with the beard, you look nothing like a servant or slave, but if you go outside, maybe you should claim you're an indoor servant."

"Ah. And inside I should say I was...what?"

She squinted, considering the matter. "How about a farmer? Hold up your hands. No, too clean."

"Are there any fighting men here?"

She nodded.

"I'll be a visiting military trainer. I admit I don't like strolling about the place in human form, but at least I know how to act in that capacity. That's settled, so we'll head outside first, I think. To find a dog."

"I'm sorry I took your rat form away from you."

He tossed the rest of the clothes back into the press. "No matter. But if you have halted my skill—the first job you should take on as a practitioner of the Arts will be to help me uncover another aptitude." *If I have one*, he didn't add.

She slipped outdoors to the kitchens to steal a loaf of bread then rejoined him in a shadowy hall near the buttery to show him a way out of the keep. At the door, she stopped, pulled the crimson ribbon from her hair and took a comb from her pocket. He leaned on the wall to watch her comb out the tumble of dark brown curls and admire the way her breasts lifted as she braided up the thick mass of hair again.

She gave him a knowing grin. He'd been too obvious showing his hunger for her. He scowled and pretended he'd paused at the door to give some unsolicited advice. "Be careful. Your awakening skills might cause trouble. I'll meet you at this door when the bell tolls two."

She shoved the comb away and retorted, "You're the one who must hide, fool. Lerae'll give out your description to every soul here."

"Fool, is it? Once again, I find it astonishing that you survived to adulthood," he said mildly. "Although...hmmm... His lordship does not like rats, but perhaps he has a fondness for shrews."

Smiling at her snort of laughter, he walked off—not too quickly, yet with a purposeful air. He didn't look back.

The caged dogs that he'd passed as a rat whimpered, but did not bark. No point in trying for one of them. Hunt dogs wouldn't be allowed to roam free. He needed a stray mutt that lived by the wattle and daub cottages. He supposed dogs like that must gather near the refuse pits. The farther from the main keep the better. He strolled and whistled tunelessly. A man wishing to escape notice would not whistle—all the more reason to do so.

He found a skinny dust-colored bitch near a garden. She watched him with wary yellow eyes but wagged her tail when he snapped his fingers. He'd pocketed most of the bread Tabica had given him and tossed a bit to the dog. She ate then quickly backed away. He tossed another scrap, this one close to his feet.

Once the animal got close enough to smell him, she allowed him to touch her. Dogs tended to like his scent, perhaps because he'd taken on so many canine morphs. As he scratched behind the dog's ear, he leaned forward and gave a tentative sniff. The dog smelled rank—likely she had rolled in some dead animal—but she held no scent of disease. This one would be fine. Instead of putting the hairs he'd captured in his mouth, he pushed them into his pocket. Hard to read books as a dog, and that was his next errand. He had to find out about the bewitching Tabica.

When he walked back toward the stone keep, the dog fell in step behind him.

He stopped and turned around and she sat down and scratched at an ear and stared out over the landscape. "Thank you for your company, hound, but I'm sure I don't need a companion."

The dog gave him a quick glance, a regretful tail flap and then averted her gaze again. He sighed, knowing the signs of a dog that's made up her mind.

No one stopped him or the dog as they made their way through the nether hallways of the main tower, the donjon. Funny how he'd been so casual as he'd first entered, more than a month earlier. He'd been so certain that the primitive shabby building couldn't hold any threat to him or his men. They came on a peaceful mission, with plans to improve the lives of the lord—the bridal price was quite handsome. Self-satisfied, civilized men helping the savages. Men from that sophisticated city of Marchosia would never be caught napping by provincial simpletons. Hey ho. No point in regretting his past stupidity.

The map he'd looked at in the lord's bedchamber had listed a scriptorium, but he doubted the current lord kept any workers devoted to work on volumes—secular or holy.

Everyone kept copies of healing books or scrolls. No doubt there'd be a copy of *Caraka Samhita*, probably an herbal. There wouldn't be many books about the Arts in this place, even under its most enlightened lord. Yet surely there'd be at least one listing of practitioners.

"Where would the documents be shoveled?" he asked the dog that had straggled in after him. Her ears lay far back on her head and she stayed low to the ground as she slunk along behind him. No doubt she'd been tossed from the place often.

Man and dog froze when footsteps clattered up behind them.

Chapter Four

"Ah good, you've brought a ratter." A large woman wearing a flour-covered garment folded her arms and examined Gil and his new companion. "She looks hungry, too. The best ratters are always hungry."

Remembering Tabica said he had the wrong air for a servant, Gil shifted backward into shadows and mumbled something he hoped sounded respectful.

"Come on." The woman bustled ahead of them. "His lordship is still in an uproar about the sick rats running wild all over the place. You'd best start in the store rooms. Don't think you can sneak off with any supplies. We keep a strict count on everything."

She left them with a lamp, a large lump of cheese and strict instructions to examine every storeroom.

In the room that smelt pleasantly of dried food and oil, Gilrohan collapsed on a dusty cloth sack filled with beans and handed the dog half his cheese. "I'm man enough to admit that I was wrong to disparage your company. Thanks to you we're welcomed like guests."

The dog fell asleep as Gilrohan searched the small cluttered room for books.

"No rats in there," Gil announced when he came out to a scullery maid sitting on a box in the corridor. "We'll keep trying."

He had success in the third room, where he found some water-logged, rat-chewed scrolls tossed haphazardly into a wooden crate. "Sad to see a life's work ruined like this, eh?" he muttered as he rubbed the dog's forehead. "Almost makes me wish I'd given a damn about this rot when I was a lad."

He held a scroll up to the lantern. The dog sighed and settled at his feet again.

One of the more recent scrolls had a listing of the names of all the known practitioners of the Arts, including the four ereshkigal and their kin. There were far fewer links in the most elite families than he'd guessed.

"In the known world with only thirty blood-line relations linked to the four? She can't be related," he informed the dog. Gilrohan began to look through the list of other practitioners of lesser skills. He paused and went to the top of the document again. The list had a recent date on it but there were five ereshkigals listed. Samanth was still on the list, had a small star next to her name and the word "reformed" next to that. Ha, reformed was a strange word for what happened to the famous Samanth.

She'd lived in his city. As a small boy he'd watched the flames leaping in the night sky the night she died. She'd been burnt to death when her river-front palace had caught fire. Even an ereshkigal could not save herself from that inferno.

He put back that simple list. Useless, really, for it had no explanations of powers and interactions. Without enough time to read more, he pocketed the other scrolls and went on to the next store-room with the dog he now called Ratter.

He finished searching the rooms, said goodbye to the flour-covered lady and, still followed by Ratter, walked up the back stairs to the lordship's bedchamber.

"Growl if you hear anything," he instructed the dog and slid under the elaborate bed, considerably harder to do now that he was a man.

He pocketed the map, the list of Lerae's other victims and left the rest. He didn't need evidence of Lerae's treachery. His king would believe him.

Tabica's heartbeat seemed too fast for her body that day. Too excited. After what felt like a life of dull servitude, something amazing beckoned. Freedom. Her mother's city of Marchosia.

Her mother had been wrong. "The simple life is best," Breena had said, trying to convince them both as they'd lain in their hut together. "This is a life worth leading, my love. I have no regrets. Later, I shall discover what skills you possess and I'll do what I can to stop them and keep you safe."

Later had not come. Her mother had died when she'd fallen off the top parapet of the keep. Like her mother, Tabica had been an ordinary servant then, but as an orphan with no inheritance to support her, she could be declared a slave. The new lord wasted no time and added her to his list of chattel.

Lerae wouldn't own her much longer. Her heart sped even more when she thought of her partner in her escape, Gilrohan, that appetizing wonderful surprise. She felt a twinge of guilt and hoped he'd managed to regain his rat form.

Toward the end of the day's work, she went to the kitchen. As she pushed the loaves of bread toward the cook who sliced them in half for the rations, Yeva appeared in the doorway, breathless and pale.

"Tabica," she spoke in a low voice. "I'll excuse the four mornings. You can have them back if you'll just do duty tonight. I've already fed him the evening meal."

She'd been looking forward to meeting with Gilrohan—she only knew how much by the depth of her disappointment.

"What's the matter?"

"My blacksmith. He's ill. I think it's bad."

Tabica felt a prickle of disbelief but dismissed it. Yeva liked her chosen mate, and fear for him would certainly make her this worried. Besides she owed her friend a debt. When they'd worked in the garden together that afternoon, Yeva had laughed at the story of the tame fesslerat throwing the lord into such a panic. She could have easily spread the story of Tabica's pet, but promised not to.

"Of course I'll take over evening chamber duty," Tabica said. "I'd be glad."

She had to wait for Gilrohan at the buttery door before she went to his lordship's chambers, and he soon came along, looking more aristocratic than ever, even though he was trailed by a skinny mutt.

"That what you're going to attempt for a morph?" she asked.

"Not yet, I think. Perhaps after the household has retired for the night." He yawned. "My friend and I have slept for the last several bells, did we miss anything?"

She told him about her agreement with Yeva.

"More of the same with Lerae?" He frowned. "I won't be able to stop the idiot."

"I tolerated him for years before you stumbled along," she said, though she was touched he wished to intervene.

"No doubt," he drawled. "Then I shall merely park myself in a quiet room—"

The echo of voices and heavy clanking footsteps interrupted him. Several of the guard coming for their evening meal. "Quick," she said and grabbed his hand.

They raced up the stairs to the lord's bedchamber.

She led Gilrohan into Lerae's dressing room and left him there with the dog. She went into the main chamber.

"Oh." Her breath caught in a gasp. She'd expected to wait in an empty room. His lordship stood by the fire with one hand leaning against the stone mantel.

"I'm not well." His voice was thick. He looked her up and down and his dark brows drew in a scowl. "Damn you. I want the woman with the chest. She moans. I'm looking forward to fucking that one once she's got a brat in her."

Tabica recalled Gilrohan's words from that morning. He'd been right. Lerae didn't want the place cluttered with his children. His father, the last lord, hadn't cared about bastards running about the place. She wasn't sure which one she despised more, the father or the son. "I apologize for her absence. Your lordship would like some healing drink, perhaps?"

"No. You never finished me this morning and maybe that's what ails me. Witch." He gave a weak laugh and threw himself across the bed on his back. His gown fell open, exposing his naked front. "Draw off the spirits through my cock."

She stifled a sigh. More of the same. She crawled onto the bed but even before she'd reached him, he began to snore.

His face was unusually pale and his lips had almost no color. Could he be feverish? She risked putting her hand on his forehead. No, if anything he was cold. She threw a coverlet over him.

The terrible snoring grew louder.

Something scratched at the door and the dog entered. Gilrohan, following close behind, stopped and frowned. He dragged a chair to the bedside, sat and leaned close to oblivious Lerae. "I smell that tranquilizer—must be a great deal of it, since I'm in human form. Did you drug him?"

"No." She rose from the bed. "I can leave. Once he goes to sleep it's— Wait, what are you doing?"

With his thumb, Gilrohan pushed up one of the lord's eyelids. When the man didn't stir, a chill filled Tabica's body.

"He's not sleeping." Gilrohan sat back and folded his arms. His usually merry eyes were grim.

"What?" she whispered.

"He's dying. Someone's given him enough tranquilizer to kill him. Yeva is my guess since she was so eager to have you here instead of her."

Tabica's mouth went dry. "No—"

He cut in, severe. "She poisoned Lord Lerae and didn't want to be caught with the body."

"Yeva is my friend. No. No, she wouldn't." She gibbered but still the truth sank in. What other answer could there be? "You're right. It must be Yeva—" She stopped as he pulled a knife from a crude belt he'd fashioned. He leaned forward.

"What are you doing?" she whispered.

His grin transformed him back into the man she recognized. "Never attempted to morph into another human. I'm not even sure it can be done but it's worth a try to keep you out of the dungeon. I've been a guest there and allow me to inform you that the cells are not pleasant accommodations. "

He sliced a lock of Lerae's hair off. "I was going to do Ratter, here." He bared white teeth and distastefully nibbled on the end of one of Lerae's hairs. "But this might work."

She sat back down next to Lord Lerae. "Shouldn't we try to save him?"

Gilrohan shrugged one broad shoulder. "Go ahead. I imagine I would if I could. Probably."

"What would I do? Touch him?"

The morphlange went into a coughing fit. At her alarmed look, he croaked, "Damned hair always lodges in m' throat." When he could speak again, he said, "Healers hold their hand just over you. Like this." He held his hand palm out, parallel to her cheek within a finger's breadth of her face. Her skin tingled; she could sense his heat over her face, invading her whole body. Intimacy.

"I'm not a healer." He spoke hoarsely and didn't move his hand.

"I feel it," she said softly.

"Mm, yes." He moistened his lips with the tip of his tongue. His eyes dilated. A ragged sigh escaped him and with obvious effort, he drew back.

She grazed fingers over her cheek where he'd almost touch her. "We're next to a man, my master, who might be dying and I want to shove you down on the bed and climb all over you, climb *into* you."

He gave a quiet laugh. "It's amazing, isn't it?"

She turned to Lord Lerae and immediately sobered. "He's even paler." She closed her eyes and held her hands close over the lord. "Should I feel anything?"

"I've never been a healer but as a patient, I've felt a sort of tingling and sometimes healing produces a sharp pain. This morning in that servant's bedchamber chamber you gave me one of those stabbing pains when I startled you awake."

"But what should I feel?"

"What did you feel this morning?"

She opened her eyes but didn't move her hands. "Other than all swollen and hot and aroused from what we did together? I don't remember."

"No, by Holy Savnack," Gilrohan yelped. "Stop. At once."

Lerae had grown paler still.

She recoiled and moaned. "Have I killed him?"

"Not yet. But look."

"No. What's happening?" Some whiskers had started to sprout from the man's cheeks. "He's...he's..."

"Turning into a fesslerat. You sucked in my form. Apparently you have managed to throw it into him."

She hated the fear she heard in Gilrohan as he muttered, "By all that's holy, you must have high blood. How can that be? I don't understand but it is the only possible explanation. You might even be related to an ereshkigal."

Something inside her congealed with dread. "And that's bad?"

"You need more help than I can give," he said.

The change took many minutes. She sat at the edge of the bed, he in the chair near her, watching her master's features sharpen, then shrink. The fur sprouted in patches. An arm and hand shrank to a tiny paw, a bizarre contrast to the large human form attached to it.

"A messy process." Gilrohan studied the man, clearly fascinated. "In me it happens so quickly, I don't notice how unappetizing it is."

At last the rat lay in place of the man. She touched it. Nothing, but soft silken fur.

"How long will he remain a rat?" she said.

"Until you change him back. I'm sure he does not contain a whiff of talent."

"Oh, no." She moaned. "I don't know what to do."

"Ah well, he's a happy rat. Look."

The near-dead man had shed his shape and perhaps the poison, for the animal scrambled to its feet and started cleaning itself.

"My Lord," she began, "I am most sorry that I have done this to you."

The animal squeaked and cringed.

"I don't understand what he's saying," she said, not sure if she was relieved or miserable. "He's just a ...rat."

Before they could catch it, the rat scurried off the bed, past the uninterested nose of Ratter the dog and under the door. Tabica started to get up but changed her mind.

"If that dog won't try, we're unlucky. Only Yeva can catch a rat."

"He'll be back, I imagine." Gilrohan propped his feet on the bed and yawned.

Tabica fell backward on the bed. "I do not understand how that could have happened."

"I told you, you have skills that are—"

"Listen. I spent the day in the kitchen and the gardens. When Hepfren came along and pinched my rear end I was angry as could be but no lightning bolts shot out of my hands. I didn't turn him into-into a gourd or a—"

A bang and a squeak in the next room distracted them.

"His lordship." She jumped up and flung open the door to the dressing room. "Oh, no. He's caught in a trap."

She reentered, carrying the rat, still caught up in a strange contraption. A wooden bar held the animal's leg in place. "Serves him right, setting up rat traps all through his chambers."

She grabbed a bathing cloth and wrapped it tight around the animal. "Don't want him nipping me. Or getting away."

Gilrohan wrinkled his nose. "You've dealt with this sort of situation before, I see."

"Yah, but never with my master. Lift the trap, please."

Gingerly, he pried up the wooden bar. She hauled out the cloth bundle containing the struggling rat.

Gilrohan went to the desk for a bejeweled chest containing documents. He set it on the bed and opened it. "This should contain his noble lordship until we know what to do."

She tossed Lerae into it and slammed down the lid. The animal scrabbled at the box for a time, but soon they heard the steady gnawing of a contented rat settling down to eat paper and the wax sealings. Gilrohan carried the box back to the desk.

"Oh my, I do hope there's nothing of any value in there." His grin was evil. "No, this is what I hope—that you manage to turn him human again so he could see how he ate his own riches."

Tabica rubbed at a small red mark on her palm—his lordship must have gotten a bite in after all.

Gilrohan reached for her hand and smoothed the tiny mark. "It's probably me, you know."

Too distracted by the finger stroking her skin, Tabica only muttered, "Huh?"

"I'm offering an explanation about why you didn't turn that odious bum-pincher into a vegetable. It might be my presence that allows you to wield your powers. That will change, no doubt, as the powers grow. But in the meantime, I think you need me close by to perform any wonders."

She squeezed her fingers closed over his. Her desire for comfort almost at once transformed into a need for more. "Please." Tabica wasn't sure what she begged for. Answers, comfort, his body to cover hers.

Even their tiny contact rendered her breathless. She met his silvery eyes that had grown dark with awareness. "How shall I explain the absence of his lordship?"

He raised their joined hands and kissed her fingers. "No need to worry. We claim ignorance."

"Mm?"

He tugged her close, up against the hard heat of his body. "No corpse, no worry."

"Oh." But she'd forgotten the subject of the conversation. His mouth lightly brushed over hers then settled onto hers. His hands stroked circles over her back, cupped her bottom and squeezed it, gently.

"Now," he whispered. "We lock the door, take off all of our clothing and discover what sort of magic we perform together. And pray that we don't kill each other."

She could only whimper as he pulled her to him. Across the room, the rat that had been her master languished in a box. They had to do something about it. Gods she had to find out what she *could* do and... Gilrohan sighed and pressed his mouth against hers.

The rat would wait. She must touch Gilrohan. Now.

Their kisses deepened. His hand, so strong and large, slid up her thigh and squeezed her bottom, pressing her hard against his erection.

"Carefully," he whispered. "We will do this so that no one shall die of pleasure."

She gave a nervous giggle. "Do you think we would die? Surely one of us would pass out. But die?"

He didn't answer right away, for he was nibbling on her shoulder and unlacing her gown to lick his way to her breast. "I must force myself to slow," he muttered, mostly to himself. "It is not a race. A leisurely feast of you. Nothing like a peasant's fast, starved fucking. This morning with you was not my finest moment with a woman, we went at each other like animals." He glanced up at her face and grinned. "No need to glare at me."

Hard to act indignant as his skillful fingers stroked and plucked her nipple. The sensation traveled deep into her, causing her to lose track of her thoughts again. She managed to draw in a shaky breath. "I think...this morning. No wonder I enjoyed it then. I am a peasant, after all."

"Ha to you, Tabica. I'm most definitely not a peasant and I more than enjoyed it," he whispered. "I want more. Give it to me."

She pulled away from him, sat on the bed. "No. We must do something."

"That is precisely what I am suggesting."

"You're absurd. I-I mean his lordship is a *rat*."

He shrugged. "And if he transforms again, he will be most uncomfortable, jammed in that box."

Tabica fought back the urge to reach for those shoulders that made even a shrug an invitation. She groaned. "Strange to think of mating at such a time."

"Yes." He bared his teeth in a devilish smile.

She couldn't look away. "I don't understand why I am so hungry for you."

His smile faded. "It's baffling, isn't it. But we are trapped here in this room for a time. Allow me to fulfill the first of your conditions for helping me escape. Oh, and we will also explore more of your education."

She held open her arms. "Show me how the civilized world makes love."

He came to her. Tenderly, too slowly, he began to remove her clothes.

Still dressed in her skirts, she squirmed away to lie flat on her back, waiting. He knelt next to her, kissed her neck and spoke in her ear. "I know many secrets about your body, any woman's body, I'd like to show you. I know how to coax you into pleasure that will last and push you so far you would come close to fainting."

His clever hands stroked her and reached up and under her petticoat to the tingling flesh of her cunt and lightly fingered her.

"Don't want pain," she said, breathless from his skilled touch and his lazy low voice. "Tell me, why do you know all these things?"

He kissed down to her naked breast. He licked it, nibbled and sucked hard.

She arched her back off the bed. The intimate throbbing between her legs transformed into demanding need.

He whispered, "We had many lessons and I learned from the best of my king's courtesans. Love play, they call it."

"You like playing with women?"

"Mmmm." His fingers stroked her, unmercifully building the pressure. A thick finger twisted up and into her. Even as he stroked her, he picked up her hand and deliberately, carefully, one by one, inserted each finger into his mouth and sucked. The hot rich feel of his mouth thoroughly encompassing each sensitive fingertip made her belly flutter.

"Yes," she whispered as he kissed her knuckles. "I like this love play. I want you to show me how it ends. Where you come from, how do I tell a man to...ohh." Her belly clenched. "To get inside me as soon as possible."

He groaned. He cursed. He pulled off his garments and tossed them over the edge of the bed, cloth and scrolls tumbling to a heap.

"You, naked," he ordered. "Now."

Her turn to torture him. Although the torment was mutual. Awareness of his intense concentration gave her goose bumps as she carefully removed and folded the remaining garments she wore. Teasing him with her slow movements.

She peeled off her last petticoat and knelt naked before him. "I have seen people mating."

"Hmm." His narrowed gaze fixed on her.

"They do it like this, sometimes." She turned her back to him rose up on her hands and knees on the bed. She twitched her bottom and only wished she could see his face as he watched her display. "Like an animal."

"Hmm," he said again, and his hands rapidly stroked up over her back, hips, behind. All over—rubbing as if he could not touch enough of her fast enough.

"So," she continued, "do your courtesans allow this?"

"Ah." His breath was fast and she could feel the blunt end of his prick graze her bottom as he reached down and forward to stroke her breasts. "Yes. Oh. Yes."

"They are on their stomachs, they open their legs wide like this, and beg you to fill them up and—"

"Tabica," he whispered. "You win."

"I win?"

"Me. You...got me. I will understand some day," an audible swallow, "how the hell you do this. You..." Warm fingers pressed her clit and behind her the hard cock thrust, blindly searching, rubbing her swollen slit. "You win."

Eagerness made him clumsy. "I give up," he groaned and with a mighty thrust plunged into her, far deeper than she could imagine he could go. Between hard shoves, he squeezed out words.

"I will...not...come in...you...dangerous...to...us."

Hearing the agony of his pleasure pushed her close to the edge of flying apart. She pushed a corner of the sheet into her mouth to keep from screaming, so her "yes, I know" came out as muffled nonsense.

"Tabica. You'll kill me." His voice sounded higher. She twisted and over her shoulder looked into his face. No more beard. Brown eyes, not grey. Thick dark brows, sharp features in a rugged face.

For a few seconds terror gripped her, nearly washing away the growing pleasure in her, for he looked just like the man she'd grown to loathe. And he was inside her. She squirmed to make him stop, the squirm made him go faster and deeper and actually shifted her own body back into growing pleasure. Lord Lerae plowed into her body. She reached back and gripped his iron thigh, dug her nails into his skin.

"No...Oh no... It's worked," she said. "You're him."

He understood. "Too late," he panted. "Can't!" He jerked out of her and pressed his damp cock along her bare back so that the pulses of hot cum bathed her skin.

Gasping, he collapsed to the side and pulled her close. "We didn't die this time." Still breathless, he managed to laugh. "So I am his lordship, eh? How sad for me. This proves once again that I am a fool to give in and touch you. Don't you dare do anything to make this a permanent state, Tabica."

The amused drawl reassured her. This was not high-strung Lerae but her own Gilrohan. Her own? Now that was amusing.

Doors slammed, marching footsteps. A whole army seemed to be gathering just outside the door. A large army of guards. In a panic, she leaned over the edge of the bed, groping to find her clothes.

"Don't move," he told her. Years of obeying that voice made her freeze.

He sighed. "And don't cringe. You merely look ready to run off and there's no need. We're safe. Recall who I am—at the moment, at any rate."

"Yes." She tried to move away but his arm remained looped about her middle.

"Don't stop touching me. We don't know if I'll be doing those peculiar shifts when your skin isn't on mine."

"But you returned to your fesslerat morph when I did not touch you. I don't understand."

He laughed, and at least that was a low warm chuckle. His lordship had more of a cackle. "I don't begin to understand either," he began, when the handle of the door jiggled.

"Blast," he said. "We forgot the 'lock the door' part of my plan."

They both sat up. Gilrohan spoke quietly. "Perhaps you should be behind me. Whisper any names I need to know in my ear."

Behind him. Yes. She slid around his naked form. They lay back down and she wrapped her arms around him hard, as if he could keep her safe. This hated body providing protection. How very peculiar.

She remembered a time she had thought the lord handsome. Dark eyes, dark hair, a fine build. As she clutched his body now, she could easily recall that first time he'd smiled at her, showing a dimple. She'd felt a small thrill in her heart.

Of course it was soon after that he'd shoved her on her knees and forced his cock into her mouth. That first time he had grown furious any time she gagged and because she'd been holding back tears, she'd found it difficult not to choke.

The door burst open. She peeked over his shoulder then dipped her head.

"The blond one is Chenote," she whispered into the dark hair that smelled like the far too familiar soap.

"Ah, Chenote," Gilrohan said, with her lord's voice. "How may I help you?"

He sounded far too urbane.

"My lord. We had word that you were severely ill."

"Grunt," she breathed. "Get angry."

"Nonsense," he grunted. "Get your lousy scratching asses out of here. Can't you see I'm busy? I want privacy."

Into the neck that smelled like Lerae, she whispered, "No, he likes it best to have people watching."

Sure enough, Chenote said, confused, "My lord?"

"I want sleep," Gilrohan corrected. "Get. Out!"

The three guardsmen bowed and left.

She discovered she was trembling. "I hope my heart will slow down some day. I wonder who made the report?"

"Yes, that's the question isn't it?" Lerae's voice asked.

She rolled away from him.

Ratter had wisely hidden under the bed when the commotion started. The dog came out now and pushed a cold damp nose into Tabica's hand. She closed her eyes and scratched behind the dog's soft ears.

Behind her, covers rustled as Gilrohan sat up. "Holy spirits," he whispered.

"What's the matter?" she asked, although she wasn't sure she wanted to know.

"Look."

The dog by the bed had been the color of dirt. Now she was white with a few dark spots. Ratter gave a hearty shake, unperturbed. But then she, or rather he, suddenly sat down and sniffed his crotch, and gave his new balls a tentative lick.

"Good thing that Ratter's a name for a male or female," she said, hysterical laughter gathering in her throat. "Oh and look, you're Gilrohan. Again."

He quickly lifted the sheet and looked down his naked body. "I am," he said and closing his eyes, let out a sigh of relief.

She moved toward him.

"No. Don't come too near."

"Oh." She sat back on her heels. "You're afraid of me."

Terrified, he thought, but the misery in her voice made him shake his head. "I simply prefer to remain a male. And I need to understand what the demons you are."

"You said it. Ereshgekil."

"Ereshkigal. But that's impossible. I said that, too." He grabbed one of the large ugly cushions and shoved it against the pillar at the corner of the bed and made himself comfortable—and far away from that pale alluring figure. He interlaced his fingers and pushed his hands behind his head to keep himself from reaching for her to comfort her and, of course, to stroke those wonderful curves. Watching her proved too much, so he closed his eyes. "Tell me about your mother. I know it is difficult to speak of this—" her gasp was indignant but he plowed on, "—but I need to know who she was. And did you know the identity of your father?"

"Why?"

"This is for the second item on your list of demands."

"Telling me about...about magic?"

"Yes, education in the Arts. Magic is generally a childish term."

A laugh echoing down the hall outside the bedchamber brought him back. He did not have time for this sort of lecture. They'd have to make plans to escape. He no longer much cared about the baron and his half-witted plans. He had to get this woman, whatever she was, to some experts. Quickly.

He spoke quickly. "Here are the barest bones of an explanation. The best practitioners only come from a few families simply because the strongest skills are inherited. I think you must be from one of these elite families. That is why I asked you about your parents. Understand? I am not being frivolous, for once in my life. "

"Are you frivolous?"

"Frequently. Not now." He forced himself to look at her again. He might be able to discern if she tried to lie to him. "Who was your mother?"

She brushed back her tangled hair. Sallos, what an erotic motion. "Her name was Breena but that wasn't her given name. My father had her change it. Yes, I know about my father. His name was Daern. He was not a slave and he might even have risen to become one of the late lord's advisors if he had been more of a schemer. Or at least, that is what my mother told me. She always loved him. I never knew him."

"What was your mother's given name?"

She frowned in concentration. He resisted the urge to smooth the skin of her brow with his finger or his mouth.

"Sam. Something like that."

He grew dizzy and cursed under his breath. "No. No. Please, not...Samanth?"

Her eyes widened. "Yes. That's it exactly. Why do you look so appalled?"

Perhaps because he was resisting the urge to fall to his knees and bow down to the daughter of one of the greatest living practitioners on earth. Or the other urge to grab her, shake her and tell her she was a careless idiot and she must get help from someone other than a lazy courtier who'd forgotten more than he'd learned about the Arts.

"Why didn't your mother tell you about herself?"

"She hated magic. It came between her and the man she loved. He never could be at ease with her, she told me. "

"Where did she meet this Daern?"

"I don't think I heard the story. She-she left her people. Snuck away to be with him."

"Staged her own dramatic death," he said, recalling the huge fire. He didn't bother mentioning that twenty-eight people died trying to go into the blaze to locate the lost ereshkigal.

"Yes, that's what she told me. She came here with her new husband who worked for Lord Leraetate, my lord's father. They were happy, though her husband...my father...hated it when she showed any sort of skill. And after a time their marriage didn't prosper."

"What happened?"

"When I was born, I had...I had some sort of glow around me. He hated me and when she refused to abandon me, he left her. He died before they could be reconciled."

He barely heard the last part of her story. Oh, holy mothers and father of spirits..."You were born with a glow?" he whispered.

She nodded. "A blue one. My mother told me once it was a horrible sign."

Gilrohan successfully fought the rising nausea of panic. "A sign, yes, but not horrible. I was wrong. Very wrong when I said it was impossible. Tabica, you are one of the four, no, now five ereshkigals on earth." He sighed and rubbed at his face. "Blessed spirits. I wonder if your Art wasn't involved in keeping me here."

"What can you mean?"

"Powerful, untapped skills can do odd things. Look for a way to emerge. I mean if somehow you knew I was here."

"I didn't know a thing."

"Yes, yes, the wrong word." To give himself time to think, he reached back and adjusted one of the pillows behind him. "Your-your skills then sensed me. And perhaps it gave your master the urge to hold me so that I would be in your vicinity. I wouldn't be surprised if it sent Master Blongette along to my cell, too."

"Who?"

"Never mind. There's no need to look so angry. I am not accusing you of being part of the scheme. I know your mind, your thoughts weren't involved in the scheme to kidnap me."

"Oh. I think I understand what you mean," she said slowly. "Do you suppose the magic is why we want each other so much? Because I need to be exposed to catch fire as you said?"

"Depressing to be manipulated by outside forces, isn't it? Or perhaps I should say forces in you that you know nothing about. "

She smiled and blushed a little. "I don't care what made me want you. I have never felt so wonderful in my life as when you touched me."

Whoops. There she managed to do it again, her direct talk of desire that seemed to reach straight into his body and trigger the full force of lust. A full cock-stand within seconds. He had to breathe in on a count of five and hold his breath to stop himself launching at her like a cat lands a mouse. He could feel his body trembling with suppressed hunger. Again?

What did the power locked in this woman's body want from him? He wished he could morph some conscious being that could discern the secrets she held. But no, too little flesh and blood in those minor forces called demons, the seat of all Arts.

He had to rely on his instincts. Sallos, what a time to fall back on them.

She stretched out onto her side, watching him. "What will we do?"

He could answer that at once. "Leave. Go back to Marchosia where I come from and find the right experts to help you. To find another ereshkigal perhaps."

At this she sat up. "Travel with you? Then you'll agree to my condition of helping me leave. You mean it?"

"Did you think I'd lie to you?"

She shrugged, lifting her sweet breasts. "I don't know you. Men lie."

He squelched his attraction to her breasts and his indignation at her words. "I don't. Not often, at any rate. At least not about important matters. Usually."

She tilted her head. "No, you are... What's the word you used? Frivolous. But not a liar."

"Thank you. I think." He climbed from the bed, conscious of her fascinated gaze.

She made a small soft sound that made him turn.

"What?"

"I really may not touch you?"

"No. I don't want to end up a nanny goat or a storm cloud."

She nodded. "I understand." A small sigh escaped her. "I love to watch you. Your body's so appealing. Much more so than his lordship's. I do like the color of your skin."

"Thank you." He picked up his trousers then paused. "What are you doing?"

She reclined on pillows, legs apart, her hand nestled between them, two fingers absently stroked the flesh between her curls. She looked down, blushed and gave a rueful grin. "I didn't even think of how I look. But...I am imagining that my hand is you. Touching me."

"No."

"No, I know. My hand is small. Yours is much larger." She leaned back and widened her legs so he could get a better view, he supposed. Or perhaps she was too lost in her own pleasure to notice how he stared. "I'm still twisted tight from before. Jangling. I did not feel release. I want..." Her eyes closed for a long moment. "I want to feel you. I need to."

"No, stop," he whispered to her and to his aching balls. Pain from too much use. Pain from more desire.

"Yes," she said. "Just once. Oh, please, just now."

He awkwardly jammed the shirt over his head and yanked on the trousers.

"Gilrohan," she whispered. "I need you touching me."

He wished she wouldn't say his name. It was worse than the dreams he'd had as a lust-crazed sixteen-year-old coming into his powers at the same time he discovered the delicious world of sex. He'd forgotten and that must be what she felt now. "We must move, woman. We don't have time for this."

Her eyes opened again, heavy and dark with lust, her full mouth damp. "Only for a moment," she begged. "Please touch me. I can't bear to think that you won't any more."

"No. We-we can't. It's been only a short while. I have no ability or interest in doing anything so quickly."

Her mouth quirked into a slight smile as she looked him up and down. "From what I see, you do, but I don't need your cock. You don't have to fuck me. Just you, kissing me, and your body touching mine. Oh, even just the heat of you near me. "

Her words were shoving him off a cliff. He pushed back. Almost angry he said, "Ah, but I want my mouth to be where your hand is playing. I want to taste you and I want that sweet musky flavor of yours to linger on my lips. I want to smell it every time I put my hand near my face because I'll have shoved my fingers and my cock so far into you I'll have captured—"

She gave a cry and her body arched up, clenching her thighs.

"Yes." She gasped and, with an amazed sob or laugh, said, "See? You do not even have to touch me."

He turned away to stop himself from once again giving into the apparently bottomless hunger for her. "Damn you and damn me. Maybe life as a nanny goat or frogspawn won't be so horrible. As long as I have some time in you before."

"I'm sorry," she said. "Oh. Gilrohan. I wish… I'm sorry I did that." The soft shuffle of the sheets told him she crawled across the bed.

"Didn't actually hurt me," he said gruffly. Fine, now in addition to wanting to throw her down and screw her, he wanted to stroke her hair and take away the scared lost quality in her voice. "Under other circumstances, I'd have loved to witness such a sight."

Her feet hit the ground with a small thump. "You sound angry or as if you're in pain."

He grunted in disgust. "We have more important things to do than worry over me or couple like idiotic rabbits in May." He shoved his perpetual hard-on to the side and made a clumsy attempt to tie his trousers. His stomach sank as he peered at the desk. "Bloody pits of hell. For one thing, it appears your baron has escaped. He chewed his way out the back of the box."

"Oh no!" She hurriedly flapped out a petticoat and slipped it over her head.

He moved to the window and his stomach continued its southward journey. "For another, I see an army amassing on the northeast plains." He squinted and then laughed in relief. In the sun he caught sight of a familiar banner depicting the wolf with a griffin's wings and a serpent's tail. "This is not so terrible after all. It is my king's army, a response to the message sent by Lord Lerae. Ah, the idiot lord ought to be glad to be a rat rather than have to face that force."

He couldn't help the pride that filled him. The king had sent at least three thousand of his forces. Of course Gilrohan knew his kidnapping was likely an excuse to bring down this nonsensical baron. Still, the sight of his king's flag gave him a surprising and unusual rush of sentiment.

A small click from her throat made him turn around.

She was fighting tears. "No, please. Don't frown at me." She drew her arm across her face. Damn her for looking lost when he needed to think.

"I'll recover in a moment. I just am-am scared of what's going to happen to this place and what's happening to me and now the lord, vanished and..." She drew in a long breath and gave a breathless laugh. "I'm frightened."

That forlorn admission did what the fascinating sight of her frigging herself to release could not. He found himself putting his arms around her and burying his face in her hair.

Stupid Gilrohan, what a stupid man, for he canted his body away, used his forefinger to raise her chin and the dark eyes fixed on his pulled him in. Her mouth, so warm soft and inviting against his, was made perfect by the slightest inexperience still lingering in her kiss.

Again ravenous for a taste of her. And another. Kiss after kiss. The quick breath fanning his cheek, the pulse under his fingers as he stroked her neck. Nothing could be more like paradise than the fit of her against him. The feel of her arms around his neck made his heart race. Blood fogged his brain and filled his groin.

And then the prickling of his skin told him something had changed. As light as a breeze brushing the hair, nothing so violent or nauseating as his usual morph. No wonder he hadn't felt it when he'd been at the edge of his release.

In his arms, Tabica seemed to grow as he shrank.

She must have felt his height change or perhaps his lips grew fuller for she pulled back, away from him. "Oh, no. You're Lerae. Again."

They waited. The still male Ratter wandered the room, stopping to scratch and listen to a dog bark outside. Gilrohan's form did not change back. He remained Lord Lerae.

She stepped close and put her hand on his shoulder. Nothing changed.

"What have I done?" She stared in horror.

"This could prove awkward," he agreed. "No need to gape at me with such fear. I'm not actually him. I'm not going to hit you. No, that's right, he prefers pinching, doesn't he?"

He held his hands out to examine the dark hair on his arms, even on his knuckles. "I wonder if when you reach your release, it causes you to—"

The heavy door slammed open. The dog scrambled under the bed. At least ten people stood frozen in and near the doorway, including the courtier he'd watched fuck the lord's sister.

The sister pushed to the front of the crowd. Close behind came her lover, the large bearded courtier.

"Adama." Gilrohan pulled up her name from his memory. Too bad he couldn't recall the courtier's name. It occurred to him that the man might actually be her husband. Quaint that they'd be happy in bed together. It also occurred to him that the man looked shocked to see him up and healthy.

Ah, so did Adama. Not a good sign.

"Brother, we...er..." She straightened her shoulders. "There is an attack brewing at last. We had thought you indisposed."

"You did? Now why is that, I wonder."

"My lord." The bearded, sister-fucking advisor stepped forward. "The army amassing on the hillside. It is King Ronan at last."

"Yes, I know," Gilrohan said. *At last?*

"We've been awaiting this moment but we—I thought you were ill, my lord, and so we have given the orders to attack."

Gilrohan stopped himself from seizing the man and shaking him. "You did *what?*"

"Do not worry, my lord, it will be an attack from the rear. The men have been sent through the forest to penetrate the forces from their unprotected side." The advisor sounded pretty pleased with himself.

"Ah, and you will drive them to the hold? Much more convenient for them to conduct a siege." Gilrohan looked over faces in the doorway and picked a young strong looking man. "You." He pointed. "Go. Send message that the attack must cease. We shall not—"

"But no," a grey-haired advisor interrupted. "This is the opportunity we've been waiting for, when you bring down the king."

Bring down the king? Lerae was a full-blown idiot. "Take the message. Go!" Gilrohan shouted. The young man sprinted away.

Gilrohan took a menacing step toward the grey-haired man and hoped his trousers wouldn't slip off his hips. "There are at least three thousand men out there," he said softly. "And how many do we have total?"

Adama answered. "At least six. You know that."

"Ah, six thousand all together. Do you have any idea how many march under King Ronan's flag?"

She frowned. "But you said we could handle them as they came in waves. You made the plans, brother. Why do you suddenly change course?"

"Six thousand against fifty thousand?"

"Fifty thousand? Not all this far north. Nonsense," said the grey-beard. "My lord," he added hastily.

"Perhaps not the whole army, but the king will have other battalions within a day's march, no doubt. We were mad to think that we could take on King Ronan and win."

Silence fell over the crowd in the doorway.

"I wonder what we hoped to gain from this," Gilrohan mused aloud.

Adama's laugh was bitter. "Did I not ask the very same question? Many times! Have you gone mad?"

"Perhaps I have," he said. "Or perhaps I've regained my sanity."

The grey-bearded advisor shot an angry look at Adama and tried to soften it as he turned his attention to Gilrohan—but his voice had turned shrill with frustration. "Are we going to allow them to march into the hold then, my lord? Simply take over?"

"Yes."

"Then, my lord, we'd best find the missing prisoner," another man pointed out. Gilrohan absently marked him as a useful sort. Nollmet—he remembered the name from the first night.

"That might be more difficult than you expect." Gilrohan wandered to the window. He tried to make out the battalion's colors. Not a familiar banner. Damn. If it had been the king's boars or the sixteenth winter-hounds or one of the others corps where he knew some of the officers, he would have been able to convince the captains of his identity. This one...might prove difficult.

A distant cry rose up. The hillside seemed to seethe and then swarm as the soldiers moved.

He cursed. "Blast! It's too late. The attack has started."

He turned to the door. "You. All. Out. I will dress and see what is to be done. Wait. Do we have any flags of truce?"

"What?"

"Flags of truce. Sky blue flags."

"What?"

Damn, this place was primitive. No time for a lecture on the niceties of battle etiquette. "You." He pointed at random. "Find the largest piece of light blue cloth you can."

The man he'd singled out turned pale, probably with fear. He waved a hand at Nollmet, who merely looked mystified. "You. Help him. Fast. Go! All of you!"

They left, closing the door behind them.

Still in command form he turned to Tabica, who'd taken refuge near the fire. "Help me dress. Find something ceremonial."

"Yes, my lord."

He gave a frustrated laugh. "I'm not your precious lord."

She was expertly flapping an overtunic of red. She stopped for a moment and smiled. "Yes, I know. Even when you are the image of him, I feel it here." She swooped her hand from her belly to her heart.

98

As she quickly tied the tunic—and untied his trousers—she asked, "So you think that Lady Adama and Sir Endor were behind the poisoning?"

"You noticed their surprise too, eh?"

"I have heard servants' gossip lately that they are not happy with the plans my lord has made. But to poison him? "

As she shoved the trousers down, her warm hand grazed his prick and leg. At once his body responded. A breeze of power seemed to blow against him.

"Am I still Lerae?" he demanded.

Squatted nimbly at his feet, the picture of a peasant, she looked up. "Yes. Even that." She brushed light fingers against the underside of his cockstand. He gasped and the desire flooded his body and mind. This had to stop. He needed his brain for matters other than dreaming of plowing into her. Or touching her or...

He wanted to tell her to take him in her mouth. Just the thought made his throbbing cock twitch up more. He swallowed, trying to push back the desire. The silence seemed to fill the air of the room with rich lust. Their gazes met but otherwise neither moved.

Gilrohan knew how to banish unwelcome tension. He began to talk. "It looks as if I want you again but I have no desire to turn into a water beetle. Although this last transformation has proved useful. We're not prisoners because of it."

She gave a half smile and with trembling hands held out the clothes. He lifted his foot so she could push on the new trousers.

His words flowed on. "All I need do is convince the troops that I'm me and that you're an ereshkigal. And we'll have an escort for you back to my home. You'll need one, I should think."

She paused as she pulled up his trousers. "I thought you said I should go to your city at once. Won't the army have to remain to finish this business with my lord?"

"What? They need whole regiments to do battle with a fesslerat? Even if Lord Lerae weren't a rodent, the discovery of you is far more important than any upstart baron."

"Oh?"

"Yes." He didn't like to think about the future. The long trek back to the city—and how hard her training would be, starting as an adult and containing so much power. But better that than staying here untutored, frightened—a slave or a pile of bones. Or a terrible uncontrolled force of nature.

She stood to tie the new trousers. A loose pair, thank goodness. He stood with his arms raised and she did the rest of her work in silence, skillfully tying and adjusting the garments. His servant again.

Her soft hands touched his skin. He could hear her breathing and taste the scent of mint. But he managed to stay still until she stepped back and he could see himself in the mirror.

He was used to seeing his reflection as a wolf, a cat, even a bird once, but it was odd to see himself as another man.

"Not bad looking, is he?" he remarked as she fastened a cape to him using an ugly and ornately jeweled pin.

"Only when he's you." She touched the indentation of a dimple on his cheek, a soft light in her eye. "You make him handsome."

"No," he said, suddenly understanding. "No, you must not love me."

She went pale. "You are thoroughly conceited, Gilrohan."

Damn, he wished she'd laugh at him or at least deny it. "Perhaps but that is beside the fact. You cannot love me. Remember that. I'll explain it later. Or perhaps someone else will. I-I should go. Please see if you can find his lordship the rat? Thank you."

Shaken, he turned and hurried from the room without looking back at her. Too much to think about. As soon as he could, he'd have to find another more skilled practitioner to take over the important duty of attendant to the ereshkigal. He hoped the gild would not decide to punish him for bedding the woman bound to be one of their most elite members.

CRSO

He didn't see Tabica over the next several bells, though he grew aware when she slipped into a room where he waited with Lerae's advisors for the Marchosian party. Even before he knew she was near, he felt a hushed expectancy inside him. Waiting for the noise to end so he could return to that important business of touching her. No. Not ever again.

From across the room, she met his eyes and shook her head. She hadn't found the Lord Rat. A problem, but he soon had a larger nuisance to deal with. His form of Lerae that had saved them now proved to be a nuisance when the advance party entered the keep.

"Captain," he said, greeting the man in the familiar Marchosian uniform. "You do not know how very glad I am to see you. Might I ask if you have any morphlanges in your company?"

The captain glared at him. "None of your northland prejudices, Lerae."

Gilrohan ushered the group into the smaller room off the main hall. No need for the entire keep to witness this.

He turned to the captain and folded his arms. "I fear you mistake me. I am myself a morphlange." He ignored the captain's extremely rude remark and went on, "I knew you wouldn't believe me and the only way I can convince you is to offer a full description of a morphlange's world to someone who'd know I am not lying."

"Produce Lord Gilrohan," the man ordered. "And we shall spare your keep."

"Ah, much as I'd like to return the noble Gilrohan to you, we've hit a slight hitch." Gilrohan said. Really, why did the mission have to be led by such an aggressive fool?

"All we require is a minor practitioner of the Arts. And you will have your precious Gilrohan, believe me."

"Why should I? We have no reason to trust you. We only come to parley for the sake of the innocents in this hold. Not for you, Lerae."

At a signal from him, the guard with him seized Gilrohan, who gave a disgusted sigh as they marched him across the room. The door opened.

"Stop," a woman cried out.

The captain sneered. "Your sister comes to rescue you."

"From what I know of her, Adama would be glad to see me go. This is Tabica." He raised his voice. "She is possibly a full-blooded ereshkigal," he ignored the gasps around the room, "and the daughter of Samanth. Tabica, meet Captain Lewter, of his majesty's first battalion. A fine soldier, but I'm afraid he does not have a career as a negotiator."

The captain, a red-faced man to begin with, turned the color of his scarlet sash. "The time for negotiations passed when you seized Lord Gilrohan, the king's messenger. And what kind of fool do you take me for? An ereshkigal? Here? And you should have done better research, Lerae. Samanth died more than twenty-five years ago. This servant—a slave I imagine—is no older than eighteen. Enough of your nonsense."

The guards tugged at Gilrohan's arms. He ignored them. "Tabica, now's the time to repeat the story you told me."

Wide-eyed and cowering as she looked around the room, she had the appearance of a cringing slave, not the strong woman who'd been slowly discovering her skills. "Sirs," she began, twisting her hands together. "He is the man you seek."

Gilrohan laughed. "Not about me, you daft woman. That's not important. Tell them about you and your mother and—"

They dragged him from the room and kicked the door shut behind them. Before they'd gone more than a few steps down the hall, a heavy thumping came from behind the room. "Here, now," someone shouted. And a guard burst through the door, half carrying Tabica.

"Ah, I see speaking did not help. Now might be a good time for you to *show* them the truth, Tabica," Gilrohan said.

She shot him a despairing look through the curtain of loosened hair that had fallen into her face.

"Don't be afraid." He spoke to her over the shoulder of the soldier clutching his right arm. "If anyone harms you, turn them into a fesslerat. Or a spotted dog."

"I think...I think there still must be some contact," she said. "Recent."

"Ah." With him, she meant. He wondered if this could be true, but decided now was not the time for experimentation.

They were marched down the stone steps to the dank prison he remembered too well. The keep's guard had surrendered up the keys to the Marchosian invaders, unfortunately.

"Put the woman in the cell with me," he told the soldiers acting as their guard. "And I'll give you the clasp on this cloak. The three of you can divide the jewels any way you please."

"What if we planned on taking it anyway?" The man on his left squeezed his arm hard. "You got no say about what happens to anything in this place anymore."

"Of course you can take it but I will point out its absence to the captain who will likely want it for his own collection and grow angry you kept it from him. Put us in the same cell, and I will remain silent about its existence."

The guards didn't respond, but he wasn't surprised when he and Tabica were shoved into the same small room. One of the soldiers held out a hand and Gil dropped the clasp into it.

The heavy iron door clanged shut, leaving the two of them alone.

He draped the stone shelf with his now loose cape and patted the spot next to him.

"Home sweet home. This is where I started out in this benighted keep of yours, although this is a more commodious room. Smells far better and has straw too. Positively luxurious. See? Things could be worse."

Tabica gave him a look and didn't sit down. He remembered another bad effect of his current morph—she wouldn't want to embrace him unless she had the powerful lust controlling her again. Sad, for touching her remained very high on his list of things he wanted to do. And since it didn't look likely that anything else on the list would come about any time soon, he had hoped she'd let him pull her close, taste her lips and everything else he could put his mouth on.

As long as she didn't reach release, he suspected he was safe, or as safe as he could be in his current form. And should he be condemned for caressing an ereshkigal, he'd argue that touching her was necessary. He wouldn't add necessary for his own well-being.

She rubbed at her arms. "Why did you allow the king's men to enter the keep?"

"You forget that I'm one of the king's men myself. And I thought this plan would save lives and get you help as soon as possible. It seemed like a good idea at the time."

She shivered.

"Yes, it is cold in here. I remember that well. Come close and we'll share body heat. I promise, no pinching."

She gave a strangled sound and moved to his side.

He looked around. The straw on the floor wasn't too dank. Kicked into the corner, with the cape covering it, that would be a far better bed for two than the shelf. His cock perked up.

"So. You think you still require contact?" he said, trying not to sound too cheerful. Circumstances did not warrant cheeriness.

She nodded and stiffly leaned against him.

He resisted gathering her soft warmth close. "I can provide that. I would even help you reach release."

He waited for her to reach for him. She'd tried to rescue him from the Marchosian soldiers. A silly and wasted effort, but such gallantry and bravery, and for him. Even while she had the fierce distraction of untrained power ricocheting through her body, she wanted to save him... Had anyone else done as much for Gilrohan? What a brave heart beat in her. His own heart turned over.

"Let me hold you and make you warm."

Gilrohan gently raised the curtain of her hair, kissed the side of her neck.

Tabica felt another shiver run through her—not entirely cold this time. So many reasons for the strange sensations. She tingled with awareness of Gilrohan but also of Lerae. And that awareness bordered on fear. Release at those hands or mouth. Or cock.

Very lightly he rubbed his hands up and down her arms. "Mm," he said. "Perhaps you should close your eyes and think of something other than his lordship."

"Even if I close my eyes...it's his smell and his voice."

"Yes, I know. Should I be quiet? Difficult, but I could probably manage."

"No, please. Use different words. Oh, but Gilrohan, we should stop for other reasons. I worry about you. I don't want to change you into anything horrible."

"More horrible, you mean. Interesting that you want me to use different words." His hands moved to her shoulders and he leaned back to cup her breasts. "He would be crude, wouldn't he? A great deal of talk about fucking."

"No, none. All...up, down, harder—instructions. Like churning butter."

"So I may describe nudging into you and how wonderful it feels to be surrounded by your tight, slick warmth and feel the first echoes of your passion? And you won't be disgusted?"

"Not disgusted. No." She gasped as his fingertips lightly circled her nipples.

"I must resist being rough with these wonderful breasts. Too much like pinching. Only the gentlest of caresses. What will bring you to the edge fastest?" he whispered, talking to himself. "Because now fast is best. Someone will soon peek in here to see if we are still alive.

He shifted closer to her. "Will you sit on my lap, let me clutch you close to me, so anyone watching would not see what we did? I want you skin to skin, but this will be better than no contact. Or shall we lie down on the straw with the cape covering us?"

The pictures of these plans clearly aroused him for his voice grew rougher. No, not his voice. Lerae's.

She averted her face as he pulled her closer and tried to get at her mouth with his.

His fingers slid between her legs and despite everything, she moaned and rubbed against him. He already knew how to touch her.

"But you're drenched," he breathed. "You are ready for me. Just climb onto my lap. Facing me. With your legs around me. I apologize for being in a hurry. We need to get out of here." He gave a soft laugh. "Yes, all right. I admit it, I need to get into you. I want to earn my punishment from the gild."

Easy to ignore his odd jabbering about punishment as his fingers made the waves grow and tighten in her. She gave a soft groan but didn't move.

"Oh. So. This is enough for you?" He pressed his finger high into her as his thumb still made the circles on her clit.

"Perhaps." She arched up to his hand. Yes. It would be enough, and she wouldn't risk hurting him. She clenched her muscles around his finger, working her pleasure from it.

He gasped. With his other hand, he worked the laces of his breeches. In a thick whisper he begged, "Please. Make me your mount, Tabica. You ride me. I'll remain still while you take your pleasure. Perhaps you can ride me back into my own body. Oh gods, I don't care, just please. Own me."

"No one owns you. I remember that." But his begging proved too much for her. She moved away from his hand, spread her legs wider and slid onto his thighs. With a grunt, he lifted her up and brought her back down on him. Impaled.

Both shuddered and went still. She wanted to writhe, but did not move, for at that moment heavy footsteps stopped outside the door.

Two trays came clattering in through the small hole. A soldier peering through the small upper hole chuckled. "Hey, what's going on in there?"

"We are staying warm by huddling together." Gilrohan spoke with great dignity. "Might we have more blankets?"

The door rattled and opened. She twisted to look over her shoulder at the two guards, one of whom wore a broad smile, the other a curious frown. Tabica felt thankful her skirts covered their joining and the disarray of his trousers.

Under the curtain of clothing, air breezed over her wide open thighs and very damp pussy.

Gilrohan pulled her closer to his chest and subtly moved farther up into her, blocking the chill—and stirring the ache. "Ride me. I am your horse," he breathed into her ear. "Shall I neigh? It would be best if you will transform me in front of these gentlemen. I'd rather be a smart horse than this stupid lord. Although I suppose you'd be on me upsidedown." A silent laugh shook him, causing him to move in a very interesting manner inside her. "Well-hung would not begin to describe that—for both of us."

The guard tossed the blankets. Gilrohan's body jerked as he caught them. She gasped and clutched at him.

"Whoops," he whispered, wrapping an arm around her. "Don't fall off. I would not offend my king's soldiers nor will I put on a show for them. So undignified."

Tabica pressed her head to his chest and stifled laughter. How could he talk so much and such nonsense? And how could he remain so entirely hard within her? She felt her face suffused with blood but he did not seem to care that they were joined in front of these men. Perhaps he had inherited Lerae's exhibitionism when he took on the baron's features.

From the corner of her eye, she watched one grim-faced of the guards cross his arms. As he shifted, his scabbard clinked against his mail. "The captain is searching the castle for your prisoner. He'll return for another interview with you at the next bell, so you better remember where you stashed Lord Gilrohan. Oh, and we're moving her out of here before then. Better have your fun while you can."

The door slammed shut and they were alone again.

"*Lord* Gilrohan?" she began but broke off into a moan as he pressed far up into her.

With a shuddering breath, he wrapped a moth-eaten blanket around her shoulders making a cocoon for them.

"This is most likely our last time together," he whispered. "I wish I had that huge bed again. I'd put you down and kiss and worship every inch of you. I'd keep on kissing you even after you turned me into a newt."

She wrapped her arms around his torso and rocked. "Kiss me," she said. "Whatever part of me you wish."

Lord Lerae's lips and tongue, but she no longer cared. She rocked on him, wanting more as always.

Under the layers of blanket and skirts he, grasped her bottom with both hands and skillfully directed her movements.

"Yes," he said. "Put your arms over my shoulders. I will carry you now."

She let him hold her weight and pump up and into her. Harder, the blinding twisting was nearly on her. The soft explosion built in her. She could not hold still, but had to wiggle on the exquisite hard man beneath her. Lerae? No...

"Gilrohan," she panted. "I am near. Let me go. I don't want to hurt you."

"Hush." His grip on her was too much. He arched and drove deep into the already sensitized part of her. His lips warmed her neck as he kissed her, licked her skin. A moment later, his breath on her damp skin made her shiver. Oh, the tingling heaviness filled her and she couldn't escape him and the heat even if she wanted to. She couldn't pull away and her body froze as the ripples pulsed through her, expanded and turned into a storm of waves.

The wall. As the waves of ecstatic release flooded her body, she reached over him and pressed her palms to the rough stone wall of the cell. She gasped through the surges of pleasure, craving more—but she forced her body to stop the blissful waves. She wouldn't haul Gilrohan into the strange loop of overpowering heat again. He cried out and pulled her down onto him. "Tabica. Don't let go of me."

She wrapped her arms tight around him as the tremors shaking her body died away. He slid sideways and collapsed at an awkward angle, dragging her down with him. For a horrible long moment, she thought she'd killed him, but then felt the rapid thud of his throat's pulse against her cheek. She reached over her shoulder to twitch the blanket over them both then closed her eyes. Fear of the future, awareness of her newly unearthed powers drifted away, leaving nothing but Gilrohan to fill her senses and mind. The slow in and out of their breathing combined and for a blissful moment nothing else mattered.

A moment, an hour or a day later–she didn't know or care—she woke to a soft low whistle near her ear. "This should serve to convince even that fool of a captain. Oh. Hello, Ratter. You smell dreadful, stupid dog."

That was an understatement.

But not only did the air reek—there was something wrong with her vision, too. She opened her eyes and then shut them again for the brightness hurt. "What is it?"

"Gold. You turned the walls to a sort of gold that glows." He wrinkled his nose. "But I think the door might be...Yes. It's now a pile of very dead fish. Ratter's just been having a snack. She—he, I mean—has come in to say hello."

Tabica lay sprawled on top of him as if she'd been thrown there. Gilrohan tucked his chin and smiled into her face. He remained the image of Lord Lerae, but with more warmth in those dark eyes than she'd thought possible.

She rolled off his body and stiffly rose to her feet. His trousers lay open, exposing him from navel to knees. She moved to help him.

He sat up and pushed her hands away. With an unusually solemn manner, he said, "No, your days as a servant are over. Soon they will come and at last understand who you are." He stood and began to tie the trousers. And as he reassembled his clothing, he talked, curdling her blood with a description of the sort of life she might expect. She'd be joining a world of formal ceremonies and solemn rites.

"No," Tabica said for the third time. She scooped up the cape and automatically began to fold it. "I will not become some sort of grandmaster of magic. Ridiculous. And these ereshkigals sound useless. No wonder my mother ran away. An altar in a temple. For me? Nonsense."

Gil managed a smile. "For you. Even the king will visit it."

"What about you? Will you visit?"

He took her hand and kissed her palm. An echo of that passionate loveplay on her fingers. But he must make her new life clearer to her. "Yes. I will pay my respects." He drew in a deep breath. "I imagine I will have quite a bit more sway in court because I discovered you."

"What does that mean?"

Gilrohan considered the question. He'd have more influence over the king and no doubt gain a larger stipend. Perhaps he'd even receive another couple of estates—chances were he'd be given this blasted holding of Lerae's no matter what he did to dissuade Ronan. In other words, he'd get nothing of any consequence to him. Nothing he cared even a snap of the fingers for.

"I will have anything I desire, I imagine," he said at last. A lie since it turned out he desired her. "Riches and all the power a man could ask for."

She made a rude peasant's noise with her tongue. She might well have gone on about the subject but at that moment someone shouted, "Holy demons above."

The astonished soldiers stood slack-jawed in the doorway. The pile of dead fish slithered around their ankles as they waded into the cell.

"Come now, admit it," Gilrohan said to her as he pulled her past the guards and started up the stone stairway. "You will treasure the sight of those gaping faces forever."

Chapter Five

The captain refused to apologize, but he did request the presence of a lieutenant who was known to possess skills as a morphlange and mesmille.

"Mesmille?" Tabica asked while they waited in a small chamber for the captain to bring the team of interrogators to them. "Bah, I have so much to learn!"

"You'll do fine. A mesmille is capable of strong hypnotic skills. My guess is he'll get me under and find out I am who I say I am. When he tries anything on you, he'll get a good blast of power."

"But I need the contact," she began.

"If you or the powers in you feel threatened, I'm sure by now you won't need me. You have caught fire, my lady."

"Don't call me that. Then why didn't I do some magic—excuse me, show my skills—when the captain threw us into the cells?"

"You must not have felt threatened, my lady."

"No, I mean it, *stop* calling me that," she said with an exasperated snort. She played with the end of her braid.

"Yes. I think you're right. I must have known we'd be fine. I knew you'd figure something out."

"Me?" He laughed. "I'm just a morphlange who might have lost his skill."

She touched his shoulder. "They'll fix you, whatever I did, I'm sure they'll fix it."

He grabbed the fingers grazing his shoulder and held them to his cheek for two heartbeats. "Tabica. I have no regrets. Granted, I want my old self again, but I wouldn't exchange a minute with you—even to be that handsome demon of a gent again."

For the first time since they'd met, her eyes filled with tears and one spilled over. He gently wiped it from her cheek with his thumb and he grinned at her. "I look that dreadful, huh."

She sniffed hard and glared at him.

The military party reentered. Tabica shot Gilrohan a wide-eyed look of horror when they all gave her a deep obeisance. They turned and gave him an abridged bow.

"Get used to the genuflections and the 'my lady's'," he said before he was led away for an interview. "Once they hear your story, they'll be groveling on the floor. My lady."

Before night fell, she was surrounded by men and women who pummeled her with obsequious questions and requests. Could the Lady Tabica please touch this kettle, brush her fingers over that stick of wood?

The title of Lady Tabica made her laugh at first, but no one laughed with her. She tried to obey their requests but through many long attempts, the kettle remained black, the stick, dull and lifeless.

She had some success once when she closed her eyes and imagined Gilrohan his head back, his white teeth bared, his face twisted in intense bliss, as he reached his release. The heat of longing tightened her belly.

"Aha!" said the woman who sat at her feet. "Yes, this is promising."

The stick in Tabica's hand turned into a small flowering bush.

The next morning she tried to find out what was going on. The men and women who'd been assigned to her care didn't know anything about the manor, her home, so she only heard through bits of gossip that Adama and her husband were to be left as the caretakers of the barony—temporarily. And a contingent of soldiers was to be left behind to make sure they did not get up to any fancy ideas of keeping permanent hold of the lands, manor and village.

The fesslerat Lerae had not been found.

Tabica picked at the fibers at the end of the satin cord around her waist. Her keepers had ransacked the whole keep for the best of its garments. She suspected the lavender gown she wore had once belonged to Lord Lerae's late mother.

She got up from the table where she'd been drinking some tea from a cup she hadn't been allowed to touch the day before. She wandered to look out the window. "Why doesn't anyone care that Adama and her husband might have tried to murder her brother with poison?"

A high ranking Marchosian attaché who'd been assigned to be Tabica's main servant, looked up from some documents. "This is a violent region and they have their own sense of justice, my lady."

Tabica gave an impatient laugh. "You forget, this is where I grew up. I don't think we treat attempted murder so lightly. Even of a monster like Lerae."

The attaché dropped the papers and rose at once. "I beg pardon, my lady." She made some soothing remarks about justice under the king, and Tabica knew the woman didn't care two sticks about the matter.

Tabica leaned on the windowsill and stared out over the undulating hills. Soon she'd leave this place and what happened in the keep, the small world she'd always known, would be of no importance in her new life. Gazing over the rolling green landscape her mother had loved, she apologized to the ghost of Samanth. *But you were wrong, mother. The simple life combined with my magic would have killed me eventually.*

CR&SO

Her keepers announced that they would form a caravan to Marchosia that would leave on the morrow.

"I will say goodbye to the people here." She'd already learned that if she asked, they'd find a way to get to the answer no in an overly anxious and polite manner. If she announced her plans, they did not dare refuse her.

In a hall outside the buttery, Yeva met her and pulled her into a hug. At least one person on the planet treated her normally, but...

"You knew that Lord Lerae was poisoned didn't you, Yeva? Why did you want me to get the blame?"

Her dramatic friend at once burst into tears. "I didn't mean to make it so you'd be blamed for my lord's death. I didn't know what to do." She wiped her eyes on her sleeve. "I was so frightened. He came in and took the packet from my hand and talked about killing Lerae—and killing me if I said anything. I thought to myself that if Tabbi saw the lord, she'd make sure he'd recover. I didn't want to say anything more."

Tabica wasn't sure she believed her friend hadn't tried to shift the blame, but she believed that Yeva didn't do the poisoning. "Who was he? Who took the packet?"

"Chernote. He put the extra powder in."

She sighed. "You were right about one thing, at any rate. I did help Lord Lerae recover. Unfortunately I turned him into a fesslerat. "

She told the story to the astonished Yeva, The tale would spread around the keep and surrounding buildings within hours. The question was—would there be a massive killing of rats or would they gather the rats and treat them with luxury as befitted the baron?

She wished she'd find out. But no, when she tried to tell her main attendant about Chernote's guilt, she could tell the news would likely be dismissed as provincial nonsense.

"If your ladyship pleases, we would deem it best if we were to depart as soon as may be."

How Tabica hated this horribly humble manner. Groveling, just as she'd had to do for years. Telling her she would leave, but disguising it as a request.

"Send me Gilrohan," she ordered. Ugh. Shades of Lerae, but she had to speak this way.

"He is to remain here, my lady."

Not if she could help it. He'd promised to travel with her and despite her new preemptory manner, these attendants of hers intimidated her. She needed all the help she could get. Drawing in a deep breath, she issued an ultimatum. "I shan't leave unless he comes too."

CRSO

The party assembled at the front entrance, horses stamping and snorting impatiently.

He wasn't there. "I will ride with Lord Gilrohan," she announced, ignoring the wave of nausea. Why wasn't he there?

The attendants twittered at her. They knew she could not ride and so they had picked Lord Lerae's best carriage for her, a gleaming black and gold creation.

"It will make me sick," she told them, though she had no idea if this were true or false. She'd never so much as ridden in a farm wagon out to the manor's most distant fields. During harvest, chattel like her had to walk.

"My lady, if you would ride postillion, might I suggest that a well-trained soldier would provide a better—"

"No. I trust Lord Gilrohan."

At that moment, he sauntered into the group, leading a large bay-colored horse. He still wore the dark face of Lord Lerae, though the familiar features appeared considerably less suave than usual for he looked as if he hadn't been shaved in days and his eyes were rimmed with red.

"So you're causing trouble?" he asked as he drew near.

"Thank you for not calling me my lady." She grinned with relief. "Yes, I am. I'm not leaving without you."

She could not tell if he resented her or was relieved. Both, perhaps.

"You're adjusting to giving orders quickly," he grumbled. "Damn. I'll have to get a different saddle."

He'd recovered his fine saddle from the keep's stables but had to give it to a common horse soldier—who was delighted with the elaborate carved thing that wouldn't fit two riders.

When it came time to mount, Tabica eyed the snorting, ear-twitching animal with misgiving. "I've never ridden one of those."

"Come on." He leaned down from the horse. "Put your foot on mine and I'll haul you up."

After she scrambled into the spot in front of him, he looped an arm around her and she settled back against his wide chest, at ease for the first time in hours. As long as she didn't look down and see how far off the ground they were, she'd be fine. She closed her eyes and listened to the shouts, the jingle of the tack and steady thud of the horses in the ridiculous parade that made up her retinue.

Someone from the back of the group bellowed, "Hey, get away, you mangy mutt. Go home."

Tabica started and opened her eyes when Gilrohan wheeled the horse around and shouted, "The dog is mine. Leave it alone."

"Yours, Lord Gilrohan? But it's so ugl—"

"It's mine."

Another closer voice spoke up. "But Lord Gilrohan. Lord Lerae is well-known for having the best hunting beasts in the north and you of all people deserve his pick. But that is obviously nothing more than a scavenger. See how it cringes and—"

"Yes, I'm sure a man of my stature deserves nothing but the sleekest finest hunting dogs. Never mind."

She smiled. "Poor Ratter has had a terrible time of it lately, hasn't she...er, he?" She risked her balance to glance back and see the dog trotting along near the retinue—turning into a skulking shadow when anyone came too near.

As they rode, she and Gilrohan argued in an undertone about sleeping arrangements. "No, I will not sneak into your tent," he growled. "And you stay out of

123

mine. Do you know the penalty for harming or defiling an ereshkigal?"

"No."

"Neither do I. No one does. When someone is stupid enough to attempt such a thing, the powerful families take care of the problem and the culprit is never seen again. Poof. Gone who knows where. Bad enough I've got the face and form of a cowardly vulture of a baron, I'm not interested in—"

She interrupted. "Yes, I see. I'm sorry. I didn't know that there were penalties. There is so much I don't know." She wiggled and resettled against him.

His hand, wrapped about her middle, surreptitiously crept under her voluminous traveling blouse. The long fingers gently rubbed her belly. After a while, he said, "On the other hand, there is the fact that holding you like this might drive me mad. Perhaps I should take my risks with the fami—"

"No, I won't let you risk—" she started and began to laugh. "We will always do this, won't we? You will say no to my pleas, and I will say no to yours. We are a sad pair."

He grumbled something deep in his chest and she leaned backwards, not wanting anything, not even air, to come between them.

As she'd hoped, he described the rules of behavior in a straightforward manner.

"Anyone below your rank, you merely nod acknowledgement. Eh, by Sallos, I suppose that means the only people you'll bow to will be the other ereshkigal."

The four other ereshkigal. She wondered if they would be pleased that Samanth's daughter had been found. Perhaps they'd wish she'd remained in obscurity.

When they paused for rest periods, he showed her how to eat and walk. She wasn't the only one to burst into laughter as he minced along imitating a fine lady.

CRSO

Too soon they arrived at the great walled city of Marchosia, which spread across the hills to the horizon. Tabica had an impression of too much light reflecting off golden turrets, white-stoned towers, pillars and shining water splashing in fountains. She'd grown used to Gilrohan's words emerging in Lerae's voice but still it was odd hearing his lordship point out the details of the city Lerae'd never visited.

"What's that?" She pointed at the largest building she'd ever seen. Many stories high, it nearly blinded her with all that gold and marble, though she liked the magnificent statues of animals placed all along its roof and walls.

"That's the guildhall for the Practitioners of The Arts. It's an extremely exclusive society run by members of the top five families. You'll be in a governing role, no doubt."

She felt slightly sick. "No. I can't imagine. The outside of that place makes me want to run and hide."

"Ah, perhaps I'll come and hide with you." A hint of wistfulness had crept into his voice.

"I wish you would."

He didn't answer. For the last day, he'd lost much of his usual informal air. No more sweet touches on her skin. Standard bland formality replaced his easy air. Both came naturally to him, she suspected. One she loathed.

When they arrived in court, his manner had changed over entirely. He gave her an elaborate bow and excused himself to go to his quarters. "The general will present you to the king, my lady."

The general bowed and scraped and mumbled incoherent lines about honor.

She gave him a nod and turned back to Gilrohan. "What are you going to do? Oh. I know. You're going to find a cure for the face you're wearing."

He wrinkled his nose and for a brief instant lapsed back into his old manner. "Yep. The power has ebbed and I'm still stuck." He kissed her hand ceremonially and did not meet her eyes. "Goodbye, my lady." The finality in his voice made her want to run after him when he turned and walked away. Instead, she allowed the deferential general to escort her to the hall.

She followed Gilrohan's instructions and only dipped her head to the king, a portly man who would have been unremarkable had he not been clothed from crown to heel in jewels and white fur. His ordinary appearance was some relief, at any rate.

He, of course, bowed low and kissed her hand. "We beg of you to consider our court your home," he said without enthusiasm.

Thanks to Gilrohan, she knew what she should say. "Thank you for your kind offer, sire, but I think it best to find a teacher as soon as possible."

The king gave the first real sign of a smile. She didn't feel insulted—it couldn't be easy having an untrained ereshkigal wandering the halls of your home.

"We will provide you with all you need for your travel to your teacher. Have you one in mind?"

Gilrohan had said that she should get suggestions from the king, let him feel like he had some say. She wished she could remember the rest of that advice. She brightened. One way to remember.

"I would take leave of my friend Gilrohan," she said. "He said he had some ideas."

"Ideas? Gilrohan?" The king hooted with laughter. "He's a charmer and a dealer. Not an idea man."

She didn't join his laughter.

"Well, then," the king turned to one of his aids, "you hear the woman. Find Gil. Fast."

A few minutes later, the page announced that Gilrohan entered the council chamber. The king pursed his lips and looked the form of Lerae over. "What? He's not his usual entertaining animal? Who's this dark and beaky man? You in trouble again, Gil?"

Tabica pressed her lips tight to keep from voicing a protest. This king did not value his faithful servant enough.

Gilrohan merely smiled and bowed. "Yes, sire."

"We shall hear your latest amusing story after we have finished our business for the day. You're wearing riding boots. You off somewhere?"

"With your permission, I will visit the estate of Lord Andras to be a petitioner, sire. I hope he could help me take back my own form."

The king clapped his plump hands. "Good plan. If your ladyship does not mind, I would ask you to seek his aid. I have been told, my lady, that he will offer private tutelage. He is at his estate. You, Gil. Go on, find out."

"Thank you for the wise suggestion, sire. I'll go with Lord Gilrohan," Tabica declared.

She wasn't sure if the king looked pleased or snubbed that she would leave right away, but he accepted her wishes with a regal bow of the head. This taking control of her own life held some appeal after all.

Gilrohan frowned.

As she left the council chamber with him, she whispered, "Who is Andras?

"An ereshkigal, my lady, the most powerful—after Lady Samanth disappeared. You can have fun playing with my king, but don't think Andras will allow you to be in command." His dry amusement held a note of contempt, which stung.

She raised her voice and addressed the attendants in her entourage. "Allow me a few words alone with Lord Gilrohan."

They vanished and she looked into his hot, miserable eyes. "Please don't be angry, Gilrohan. "

He shrugged. "My lady, you are mistaken. Who am I to be angry with an ereshkigal?"

She resisted the urge to shake him. "Should I stay back then? While you go speak to Andras?"

He closed his eyes and knit the dark brows she'd once hated. "No," he said at last. "I think you are right to go at once. If he can't help you, he'd be certain to send you to someone who can."

"Tell me why you look upset."

His sharp laugh startled the man near them in the hall. Gilrohan must have noticed the man's curiosity for he led her along complicated rabbit warren of passages. After ushering her into a stuffy room that might have been a large closet, he turned. She thought he would speak, but instead he pulled her into a kiss. Angry and frantic at first, his kiss melted into pure sweetness.

Her limbs grew heavy with longing as she tasted delicious pleasure. The hunger in her belly woke at once. Her hands ached to touch him, but because he wore heavy travel garments, she could only stroke the swathe of skin at the nape of his neck. He broke off the kiss and stepped back, panting.

"That. That's why I'm upset." His voice cracked. "I think of you and your body every moment of every day and I am useless. You turned me into an ocean of unquenchable desire."

She wanted to retort that she suffered the same ailment too, but she ignored the twinges of her body as she examined his angry, drawn face. He had rescued her from slavery and in return? She had ruined this man's life—turned him into the image of a brutish thug, and now somehow snared him in a trap of lust.

Misery twisted her gut as she understood that he truly had to get away from her. Ignoring the sensation, she spoke. "We should go now. Without delay."

His face lost some of the dark anger. "I shall meet you at the fore gate. One of your attendants will show you the way. Oh blast, we'll have to find those keepers of yours first, won't we?" He opened the door and waited for her to leave. As she passed, he muttered, "Forgive me for acting like an overwrought idiot, my lady."

"Only if you stop calling me that."

His smile seemed genuine. "Tabica." A soft whisper of her name.

She stopped, but he said nothing more. Silent now, he led her to the small group that waited. He bowed, swiveled on his heel and was gone.

CRSO

Andras's manor lay near Marchosia so their journey took less than a day. This time, thank the heavens, Tabica didn't insist on riding with Gilrohan. He did not fancy embarrassing himself by howling like a wolf or attempting intercourse on his startled gelding. He should have regretted revealing his pain but he knew that she would not intentionally use it to her own advantage. She hadn't been in the court and didn't understand the game of holding the advantage, even over your bed partners. He trusted Tabica, he realized with some surprise. Her skills, on the other hand... Gilrohan was smart enough not to trust that untrained power.

Lord Andras kept a greater numbers of servants than even the king, so a veritable parade of starched footmen led them to the gilded reception area, where Andras himself met them, then dismissed the army of footmen.

Dressed in the black and scarlet ceremonial robes of an ereshkigal, the dapper old man was stuffy, bureaucratic and terrifying. As a court official, Gilrohan had seen him at state dinners at the temple, including the annual fete in Andras's honor. He'd forgotten the power of the ereshkigal's presence. Even the man's trimmed white beard seemed to bristle with fierce restrained strength and the thick glasses shone giving him the appearance of a malicious owl.

The old man studied Tabica, up and down. "So you've shown a skill at transformation."

She nodded.

He stroked his neat beard with a manicured hand. "Demonstrate."

"But I don't know what I do."

"Concentrate from the rib region I think."

"On what should I—"

"Transform me."

"But I do not know what will happen. You may end up a–a slab of beef."

He smoothed the ermine stripe on the shoulder of his robe and shuffled closer to her. "I doubt it. Go on."

She turned pale, but held out her hand, palm up.

Andras clicked his tongue. "You're not a healer. You taught her this, Gilrohan?"

Startled that the man would recognize him, Gilrohan began, "Yes but I didn't know any oth—"

"Obviously. I recall that Blongette frequently moaned that you would not apply yourself." The old man turned his attention back to her. "You don't need any hand flapping nonsense. Oh, and another thing. From what I can comprehend, you will need to stop working from your womb. We will soon concentrate on controlling the sexual zone. For now I think you had best use your bloodstream. Simple beginner's work. Once tamed, your womb will be a mighty source." He scowled at her belly censoriously, but with the corners of his mouth tipped in a smile.

He leaned close to her and whispered in her ear for far too long. Gilrohan wanted to howl.

Andras stepped back. "Those sexual powers are too strong and capricious for the untrained. For now, you will work from under the ribs, if you please. As I just described."

She grazed fingers over Lord Andras's shiny forehead.

The gray-bearded man shimmered, disappeared and in his place stood a tall, dapper man with jet-black hair and a neatly trimmed black beard.

"Very good." He straightened his back experimentally and rolled his shoulders. The ereshkigal robe, which had engulfed him, now hung from his straight shoulders adding to the impression of barely contained strength. As if the old bugger needed to exude any more power. Andras nodded. "Very good."

He squinted, took off his glasses began to polish them, then blinked. With a casual underhanded throw, he tossed them into the fireplace. "Yes, I will certainly help train you. And I'd say you'd already paid your tuition for my troubles. I've spent some time attempting this. Beginner's luck, I'd say."

The man's smile contained a smirk that made Gilrohan want to knock him down, ereshkigal or not. He no longer looked like an owl. Now he resembled a shining, clever raven—only far more handsome than one of those birds—and his smile at Tabica contained a touch of wolf.

"Well then, Lady Tabica. Shall we return this man to his original appearance?"

She stepped forward and hesitantly brushed a finger over Gilrohan's temple. The wave of power washed over him. Perhaps this training would come easily to her. That was something to be grateful for, he supposed.

"No," she said, and tilted her head mournfully. "At least not entirely."

Demons, what could that mean? But before Gilrohan could protest, Andras gave an impatient grunt and tapped Gilrohan's arm with his palm.

He grew dizzy and nauseated as he usually did during a morph. He heard Tabica sharp inhalation but he didn't panic, for her face lit up with a wide smile. "Thank goodness. Oh, I have missed seeing you and—"

"You may go, Gilrohan," Andras interrupted again.

Gilrohan, dressed in clothes now slightly too small for him, awkwardly bowed. He wanted to drag her with him. Find a room to show her how he wanted to say goodbye.

She drew close to his side but did not touch him. He wondered if she feared he'd explode into another rage if she did. "You'll visit, won't you?" she asked.

"We'll summon you," Andras said, watching Tabica with that bird of prey look of his. "Goodbye."

She walked Gilrohan to the door of the large reception chamber. "You woke me up and set me on fire," she said. "I will be grateful forever."

She drew him down to her for a soft, fast kiss. He somehow managed to pull away. But when he bowed again and walked off, it seemed to him he left behind joy.

Chapter Six

Tabica's lessons were difficult and left her exhausted. Master Andras did not allow her free time. "You have too much to learn."

She made progress, but not consistently. She would easily comprehend the shape of a particular lesson, but as she visualized, something like a cloud would shift in her vision and some strange jolt would occur as if a giant hiccup interrupted the natural flow of her power.

"Engorgement. Builds too much and...boom. Small discharges of unwarranted power." He glanced at her lower belly and raised his dark brows. She felt an answering clench and tingle of interest as if her womb had a mind of its own. Demons, she would force her body into submission. No. Not *him*.

As if he heard her, his lips quirked into something resembling a smile.

At night the hiccups were worse. She awoke from a dream of a naked Gilrohan, his cock filling her. As she stumbled from the bed, she tripped and tried to push aside the slipper—only discover she'd tripped over a root, not a slipper. A huge tree had sprung up in the chamber. She sank to her bed, cursing under her breath as she rubbed her bruised toe.

Her effect on the creatures around her proved to be unpredictable. Andras purposefully picked a dour sexless creature for Tabica's personal maid, but the woman must have spent too many hours in Tabica's presence. She was discovered naked in the arms of a cook's assistant.

Tabica took riding lessons and the grooms who helped her had to take days off after spending too much time with her. The one who helped her on and off her horse seemed the most badly affected. He began singing ballads day and night.

An elderly stallion kept in the stall next to her docile mare took to plaguing all the mares in the stable. None of them were interested—except the mare Tabica rode nipped at his mane when they stood side by side in the stables.

Andras responded to her disturbances by piling on more work on her. Good. She wanted to learn as much as she could. If she could learn to control her power, perhaps she could control her life—for the first time in her memory. Freedom beckoned.

The lessons exhausted her, and yet at night she could not sleep and walked the large manor house to work off tension.

She came into the library, a magnificent room of books and scrolls and intricate parchments, to look for something to distract her from her restlessness.

Andras looked up from the desk where he worked. "You've come to study?" Only Andras had seemed unaffected by the aura of unrequited lust that hovered around her. Yet something seemed different in him tonight. Her stomach fluttered uneasily, even as she felt her power surge like a ball of warmth low in her belly.

She nodded and backed away. He rose from his chair and noiselessly walked to her. He had thrown off the loose ceremonial ereshkigal robes and wore simple breeches and tunic. Just as she reached for a book, he spoke.

"No. No more words for you. You need a more physical lesson. I can feel the tension in every room you enter. You still gather too much into your womb."

Before she even had time to absorb how close he stood to her, his manicured fingers covered her belly. At once she felt the tension dissipate slightly as if he'd touched a knot of muscle in a sore back. But then she grew aware of his hand. Moving over her, rubbing the soft cloth against her too aware skin. God, the tension grew tenfold.

"Concentrate on my hand, not your sex."

She inhaled sharply as his hand moved on her.

"No, not arousal." He sounded angry—and slightly husky. "Not that. Power, not arousal."

But even as he spoke, his fingers moved down and brushed her curls through the cloth.

"I am losing focus," he said, and drew in a deep breath. "Ah well. Shall we get this over with?"

"What?" she said. She opened her eyes when he removed his hand. He needed it because he now unfastened his shirt.

"Oh, but this isn't...we can't..." Her words faded as her body roared awake.

He pulled off his tunic, folded it and laid the neat bundle on a chair. "Young lady, it has been fifty years since I've lain with a woman. This reawakened youth is a confounded nuisance and if I walk into another room to be smacked in the gut by your musk and desire, I'll go barking mad."

Lord Andras, though. Oh demons. "Must we do this?" Her back pressed against a large bookcase.

He stopped and looked at her, his dark head tilted back slightly. She'd seen this pose before and imagined that before she cured his eyes, he would have peered over the topes of his glasses. "Naturally I shall not force you. But I am thoroughly distracted by you. I think it best if we get this unnecessary distraction out of the way. Furthermore you are not operating at your fullest potential. We will drain your sexual obsession once and for all and allow you to at last function from some portion of your body not aroused by carnal desire."

She stared at his chest, lightly flecked with dark hair. In the shadows cast by candles, she could see the shift of his taut muscles. Her body tightened with involuntary waves of lust.

"Oh," she breathed.

"On second thought, a bed would be more comfortable." He turned and strolled from the room. Tabica stared after the lean, no-nonsense body. "Come along," he said without even turning around. "We will banish this annoying uproar of yours and get your training properly started."

He led her to her own room, past the towering beech that still flourished in the middle of the stone floor. Either he did not want her to see his room or he didn't want his bed mussed by...strenuous exercise.

His unruffled demeanor curbed her nerves. Perhaps he was right and this ritual would free her of her restlessness. She must trust his greater wisdom and experience. "Shall I undress?" she asked. Her voice was normal enough, though her heart beat too quickly.

"Whatever you like." He sat on the edge of the bed and methodically removed and folded the rest of his clothing.

Her stern mentor, naked. On her bed. She had to close her eyes. If he were correct this would give her more control of her power.

"Come along then." He sounded impatient, as if she'd bungled some minor point of ereshkigal history and he expected better of her.

She whipped off the gown she wore and tossed it across the bed. His harsh involuntary gasp gave her a measure of satisfaction.

She climbed onto the bed and lay down near him, but not so near she could feel his heat. Would he kiss her? Mutter about her sweet breasts?

He stretched out his long body next to her, those sharp, cool eyes studying her face.

"Your power is a pent up animal. It is restless and must be released from here..." His palm suddenly covered her mound. "Yes, I have taught many young creatures. We must allow them some exercise before we try to force them to concentrate on lessons."

"Funny way to exercise," she muttered. "Will you take any pleasure?"

He frowned and shifted slightly. "Hmmm. This is not for me. You."

Was this a reminder for himself and did that mean he did not intend to penetrate her? She wasn't certain if she was glad or disappointed but then his long, skillful fingers had dipped between her legs, causing her focus to rush to the point he touched.

She cried out when exquisite sensation curled through her.

He moved closer to her, and she felt the hard length of his penis brush her leg. When she reached for him, he moved back with a hiss. His fingers still caressed her. She didn't want this but... Oh demons, she needed it.

Andras must have lost another battle, for his erection pressed against her leg again. He moaned and eagerly slid a finger into her. He groaned. "By Sallos, you are so warm and snug." Deep inside her, his long fingers stilled. "Wait. What man have you killed?"

"What?" She arched up to his hand.

"You-you are not a virgin. He must have died."

She whimpered and spread her legs wider.

"Stop. I won't be forced," he whispered. "Halt yourself. No. Stop wielding your power. Hold back. We do not come to this yet."

No. Through the haze of lust that gripped her, she understood only desire. Demons, she would never be in thrall to anyone again. Reaching for control, she would pull it all to her. She rolled her hips and dug her heels into the bed.

Andras cursed and threw himself on top of her. Awkward as he fought his unwilling eagerness, he prodded at her with his penis. She reached between them and fitted the rock-hard cock to her slit.

With a spasm, he pushed into her and then held still, quivering with the effort. When he moved in her, he'd regained his precious control and slid in and out, achingly slow. Almost as calm as he might be while conducting a lesson, he continued, "Now. The power. It grows but... Push it from your-your...ah."

She drew in a deep breath and smelled his warm skin spiced with the exotic expensive scent he wore. Her mentor? As she pressed her face against his throat, a groan rose deep from his chest and he jerked slightly as he struggled for control again.

"Slow," he growled.

She writhed under him. At last comprehending the boundaries of the fight, she knew she would win. She must or die of frustration. "No, you move. Harder. Faster," Tabica ordered.

He pushed himself onto his hands and rose above her, his face contorted with concentration. "Stop! This desire is too powerful..."

He supported himself on muscular, trembling arms and a drop of sweat dropped to her breast.

"You began this, sir," she snarled, angry with herself for allowing this peculiar incident even as she filled with longing and the dull ache grew sharper and stronger. "You will finish the way I want it."

She bucked, breaking the smooth, slow rhythm that threatened to drive her mad. He pleaded with her, panting. "Oh, no. Please. Please."

His hands clasped her buttocks tight. She felt triumph as he furiously pumped into her. "You-you," he moaned. "Control... Me. *No.* Stop."

With each frantic push, the rasping pressure inside her grew. "Now," she whispered. "Now I will release."

She reached over her head, arching her back so the sensitive tips of her breasts brushed against his writhing body. No, she wouldn't be distracted, she must find something.... And grasped a pillow. Perhaps that could take the brunt of the power that raged in her lower belly.

Some escaped from her body through her arms, to her aching fingertips. Light. She would think of something shining. She thought of Gilrohan's glowing face. The memory of his warm smile filled her and the waves hit at last, rolling through her.

Above and inside her, her teacher shuddered, made a sound of an animal gasping in pain. And the man who valued dignity whimpered once more and collapsed like a felled tree on top of her, knocking a surprised "oof" from her.

She felt his steady breathing, saw the rapid pulse in his neck. He wasn't dead or injured yet guilt struck her. The fight for control had been instinctive but part of her had gloated as she fought and overcame him using his desire for her.

"Sir?" she whispered. No answer. She managed to wiggle out from under his weight. A small tinkle of metal startled her. The pillow she'd clutched had turned into a pile of gold coins. Damn. Not the effect she'd planned at all.

She looked down at the stunned body of her teacher and realized he had not kissed her. That was a relief, she supposed—and then she wondered how he might taste. And what sort of a kiss would he bestow, flickering or thrusting? Her womb twisted. His eyelids fluttered.

No! She quickly got up and found her clothing. After she'd rinsed herself, she came back to the bed and discovered he'd rolled onto his side and watched her.

"You didn't lie to me?" His faintly disdainful self had returned. Though he lay in her bed, stark naked with a sheen of perspiration coating his skin, he was nearly transformed into the usual intimidating teacher. Yet she thought she saw the shadow of something new—anger, fear or perhaps vulnerability—in his eyes as he looked at her. "It wouldn't be considered murder, you know. We ereshkigal are allowed some leeway when it comes to matters such as death."

"Might I ask what you are talking about, sir?"

"The man who took your maidenhead. You claim he actually lived to tell the tale? Can he still speak? Walk? Function?"

"It was Lord Gilrohan." She tried not to blush.

His eyebrows shot up. "Well, well. Who would have thought it?"

He rose from the bed, stumbling slightly as he straightened. The hand reaching for his trousers trembled.

"That was most...interesting." His voice was quiet and he studied her face then his gaze, still softer than usual, dropped to her breasts.

She licked her lips, trying to resist the urge to ask if he enjoyed it or if he liked her body. She knew he'd never volunteer anything more about his experience in her bed.

He wiped the sweat from his forehead with the back of his hand then collapsed into a chair. "Gilrohan, you say?"

"Yes."

"And yet I did not sense any major problems with the man, other than the stalled morph. Amazing." He closed his eyes and tilted his head. "Amazing." Only this time she suspected he meant what they'd done together. "Did he have a...uh, reaction like mine?"

She understood he wanted to know if Gilrohan had passed out. "No, sir."

"I take some consolation in the fact that your powers are at almost full strength now." He pulled on his trousers then slowly stood and fastidious as always, turned away to fasten them. "Then we shall summon him."

"What?"

"You are still blocked. Lord Gilrohan is obviously far stronger than any in the high families previously supposed." He faced her again, but did not look at her. Instead he knuckled his eyes then smoothed his ruffled hair. "I can't be trainer and teacher. You are a thoroughbred. You require more attention than most students as it is..." His gaze returned to her breasts. He shook his head. "Amazing."

He dragged his attention away and frowned down at his immaculate fingernails. His hands trembled. "Your power grows so much. Gilrohan had best be strong. I hope he will still be able to withstand—"

"No," she said. "I'd rather have you, sir." She wouldn't of course.

Her teacher gave a short laugh. "I'm complimented, but I will summon him."

She refused to be responsible for harming Gilrohan. "Shouldn't this sort of...um...issue be solved by an ereshkigal—someone who has a great deal of magic?"

He grimaced. "Skills."

She flapped her hand impatiently. "Yes, yes skills."

"No. I do not break the horses I ride."

"Excuse me?" She wanted to demand he explain exactly what that meant. Did he intend to "ride her"? Naturally, he wouldn't answer a question like that. His small smile made her suddenly aware of her nakedness. She dragged her dressing gown from the bed and wrapped it around herself.

"I will meet with you in the morning. We can discuss it then." For the first time since she'd met him, he bowed to her. Then he walked from her room slowly, almost like the old man he'd been before he'd met her.

He didn't discuss it, however. He merely announced that a messenger had been dispatched to fetch Gilrohan.

CRSO

Someone banged on the door, waking Gilrohan after a long night of debauchery. Or at least Gil supposed it was debauchery. He'd drunk enough he wasn't certain what had gone on. Now his mouth tasted of old metal, his head pounded and someone wasn't helping matters by shouting his name and making a racket on his bedchamber door.

"Enter," he croaked, wondering if life could become any more horrifically surreal. Three weeks and he still hadn't adjusted to the court and its nonsense. He had always excelled at nonsense—that was until he'd gone on that damned mission and been thrown in a dungeon. And met her.

The man in the officious-looking page's uniform bellowed at him. Some sort of exalted messenger, probably. Gil forced himself to pay attention, and then wished he hadn't.

"What in the name of Savnack are you babbling about?" The pounding headache was no excuse for rudeness. He reached for a cup of water gulped it down and tried again. "Excuse me. You say you are from Lord Andras? Why in any demon's name would an ereshkigal *require* me?" Even as he asked, he realized it must be something to do with her. No. She would not pull him back in. Not after he'd begun to crawl out of the trap of useless sorrow at leaving her behind.

"You are to come. At once," the messenger informed him. "You are to bring at least one week's clothing."

The messenger strode from Gil's chambers without waiting for an answer. No need, for there was only one possible answer—yes, of course. No one ignored a summons from Lord Andras, not even the king himself.

Gilrohan might be summoned like a dog, but he'd come to heel when he was ready. And speaking of dogs, he'd have to find someone to watch Ratter. He took his sweet time on arranging that matter and didn't leave the palace for Andras's manor until late in the afternoon. Ignoring the pleas from his valet, he traveled alone.

Gil had the dubious honor of being met in the entry hall by Andras's most powerful servant, a grim-faced, fat steward, Wilde. One of Gil's friends, a member a high family who'd been trained by Andras, insisted the steward ate live rats for rituals. Generations of high-born pupils had dubbed Wilde the Dragon of All Terrors.

After less than an hour in the anteroom, Gil was shown into the chamber where Andras held court. Seated on a high dais, at the table stacked with documents, Andras looked like a vengeful god of clerks. Sallos, *she* sat at the impressive ceremonial table, too. The elegant maroon velvet gown made her skin glow. A copper circlet ringed her chestnut hair and her lips looked warm and soft. Gil's mouth went dry and he wondered if he would be able to speak. He'd better shift his attention to Lord Andras or risk looking a great fool.

Indeed the sharp-eyed ereshkigal smirked knowingly down at him from the dais. Under the ereshkigal robes, Andras still wore the staid clothes of an ancient, a strange contrast to his vigorous young body.

"You require my presence?" Gilrohan gave a bow and allowed himself a quick glance at Tabica. Her large dark eyes met his for a second. Demons, the life seemed to pour into him, whisper through his limbs. She bent her head to study one of the piles of papers in front of her and he could breathe again.

"I certainly do not require you," Andras said dryly. "And I'd far rather Tabica didn't, but I have less control over her than I'd hoped."

"I am sorry, sir, I do not under—"

"You will take part in her training."

"Excuse me? I'm not a teacher."

"An understatement. But your presence will be required in her bed, not for her lessons. She knows what is expected and will tell you as much as she needs you to know."

A bed partner? Gilrohan's stomach swooped with dismay and interest. He risked another look at Tabica. Now she wore a glazed expression as blank as if she were uninterested in this whole interview.

Gilrohan seethed. He'd been a puppet in the court, but at least in his own familiar terms. Now she set the stipulations. Again.

He would be a sex toy for a bored ereshkigal? No.

"I beg pardon, sir, but I must refuse," he said at last. "I have an errand for his majesty and I would—"

"Nonsense. You know that the families' needs take precedent. This is not a position you may decline."

"Nevertheless, I do refuse it, my lord."

Lord Andras rose to his feet, no doubt to issue a horrible threat.

Without permission, Gilrohan sat on bottom step of the raised platform. "I want to know why you need me in particular. Sir."

Andras grunted. "I considered using a member of my staff, but I feared the lady might kill or incapacitate him. "

Gilrohan fleetingly wondered when the miracle had occurred—Andras developed a sense of humor? He turned most of his attention to Tabica. He'd addressed the question to the higher-ranking ereshkigal, but wanted to know her answer.

Under his examination, she frowned, shrugged and shifted in her chair. Gil suddenly recognized the blank expression. It wasn't boredom. She'd donned it long ago as she performed "service" for Lord Lerae. She didn't like this any more than he did. He cheered up slightly and rose to his feet.

With a bow to Andras, he asked, "When would you need me, sir?"

"Now, I should think." Andras tapped the table to gain Tabica's attention then waved his hand dismissively at her. "Go on then. Go play."

Now that was interesting. What caused the bitterness in his voice?

"I will finish this." She again leaned over the scroll in front of her.

Time to put away the toy, then—she'll play with him later. No, her hunched shoulders reminded him she must not have planned this.

A voice at Gilrohan's side startled him. The Dragon Steward rumbled, "You will follow me, sir?"

He recalled Tabica's bitter description of obsequious orders and smiled to himself. Did she still think badly of his world? "I must see to stabling my horse and bring in—"

"All has been attended to, my lord."

With mock civility, Gil bowed to the erishkigals and followed the large steward through cavernous halls to a huge bedroom, the chamber of a high-ranking female. Tabica, the former slave.

He ducked beneath a low branch. "Why is there a tree growing in the middle of this room?"

The steward rumbled a bit before answering. "We have had some unusual occurrences of late, sir."

He grinned. No, there was no sense in hiding from himself how much he'd missed Tabica. Whether or not he'd show her was a different story. This might prove an interesting task after all.

Still in dusty boots and travel-stained cloak, he dropped onto the giant bed to wait. The silken sheets felt even smoother than any he'd lain on at the palace. "Ereshkigals," he muttered. "Blast them all."

Chapter Seven

She'd dreamed of him at night, thought of him through meals—and her more boring lessons. Now he lay sprawled across her bed, eyes closed, breathing softly. The dim light filtering through the curtains turned his hair to gold. Even sleeping, Gilrohan proved larger and far more vivid than her memory of him. Of course she'd met him after he'd spent time in Lerae's prison. Freedom suited him far better.

Should she wake him?

Circling the bed, she examined him from all angles. The long muscular legs and broad chest under the dark clothes were attractive but something more called to her. The first time she'd seen him, even in his form of a rat, she'd sensed a quality that drew her. She wondered it was her own hidden skills pulling at her to claim him. Yet since then she'd been exposed to other people with magic—skills—and yet something about him made the center of her body ping in greeting.

No sign of his superior air, no gleam of that drawling humor but the lines of his smile still touched his face. She touched the edge of his clean-shaven jaw.

He opened his eyes. The smile faded. "Your servant, my lady." He sat up. The soft leather boots and well-made dark clothes reminded her of his own high position in the world. He gracefully rolled to the edge of the bed, stood and bowed low.

"Gilrohan, just stop." She bit her lip and dropped onto the bed. She sat on her hands just in case he kept up the stupid formal manner. Or maybe she wanted to keep herself from launching at him and pulling him into a kiss. Both instincts seemed equally strong. "I-I didn't mean to have you yanked out of your life and brought here. I'm sorry."

"But I understand that I am to perform service for you, my lady."

If she hadn't seen the hard wariness in his eyes, she would have slapped him for using that odious drawling voice. She understood the necessity of hiding anger or fear too well. Gilrohan, a slave? Never. "You can't perform any service for me."

"I beg your pardon, my lady?" Still with the loathsomely polite manner, but she could ignore it now that she had decided to tell him everything.

"From what my mentor says I might harm you. My power has grown but is still not under control, you see. And I might actually kill you. We can't do...anything."

At last he seemed to soften. He touched her cheek, a light brush of the finger, but enough contact to make her shiver. His eyes closed for a long moment. "I am sure he has taken that into account," Gilrohan said thoughtfully, all traces of the drawl gone now.

"What do you mean?"

"I'm not sure. He is ereshkigal and they are excused from the usual laws. If you expressed a preference for me, this would be a convenient way to dispose of me. If he wishes me dead, I am doomed."

"No," she said. "I don't believe it."

He raised an eyebrow and she recalled his years in this world she'd only recently joined. But Andras? She shivered again, this time not with arousal. "He won't kill you. If he tries... I am ereshkigal, too. I won't let him."

His smile, warm and real, lit his face. The first real smile she'd seen for years, it seemed to her. He sat on the bed next to her. "You would save me?"

"Yes."

They'd drawn close. Oh, just a few more inches and she'd be able to kiss him.

She pulled back, decisive. "I will save you by telling you to leave. Go. I will tell him that we...that we mated and you did not succeed and I dismissed you."

"What will he do after you make this announcement?"

She tugged at the velvet gown's neck—she was not used to low necklines. "I'm not sure."

"How will you be serviced then? What will you do? Wait." His golden brow furrowed. "You and he have explored this problem of yours? Together?"

"Yes, well, it was part of my training."

His mouth tightened. "Huh. I'm not surprised. And if I leave, he'll be in your bed again?"

"I don't know. He might try to find another man for that...work. He did not seem to like it."

"I find that extremely hard to believe."

His incredulity sparked a warm glow in her heart.

"But it's true that my power is strong." She told him how Andras had fought her and eventually fainted.

He paled and clutched her arms. "You won? You forced him to lose control?"

She nodded.

His eyes widened. "Gods and demons above. You." He shook his head. "He will not have liked being dominated."

She tried to concentrate on something other than the feel of his fingers on her arms. "No, he didn't. But still. I'll figure something out—it's not your concern."

"My concern? I can think of nothing that concerns me more. Than you. " His silver-blue eyes dilated. Too late. Her body grew heavy with desire. They had waited too long.

"We still can say no," she whispered as his warm breath touched her face.

"No," he responded as their lips met.

His mouth tasted like salty honey and pure Gilrohan. She hadn't known how she'd starved for his flavor.

She whimpered with satisfaction and the urgent need for more. But not at this cost.

Tabica ripped herself away. It felt almost as painful as a tear to the skin.

His chest heaved with quick breaths and he refused to allow her withdraw entirely from his grip. "Listen. If it isn't me, someone else must help you, yes? Let it be me then."

"Nonsense. I think Andras grew impatient and tired of...my bad influence. I will manage this on my own. The power."

"Remember when you used your hand to bring on your own release."

She blushed and looked down at her shawl. "I recall."

"Have you done that again?"

Twisting a bit of the silken shawl, she nodded. "But the strange pattern has not washed away, only been altered. My master believes the only way to solve it is with another to capture and rechannel the power as it flows out of my womb. I would keep trying other methods, such as...ah...by myself."

He grinned ruefully. "I don't think you get to decide this matter. Do you honestly think he will allow me to walk away when you're not cured?"

"Of course he will."

He broke into a laugh. "Ask him."

No time like the present. She ignored Gilrohan's startled "wait, I didn't mean it". Heaving at her velvet bodice, she jumped up from the bed then strode from the room. She remembered to drop into the slow, mincing walk of a lady only when she drew near the audience chamber.

The vast and impressive consultation room was empty except for Andras and the intimidating head steward who reminded her of one of Lerae's more intimidating and evil-tempered under-cooks.

She stood at the bottom of the dais rather than trot up to her usual spot at the table. At Andras's enquiring look, she came right out with her demand. "I would request that Lord Gilrohan be allowed to return to the court. "

He put down the sheaf of papers he held and made his way sedately down the stairs to examine her. He stood four steps up, probably so he could loom over her. "Has your cure been produced already? How can this be done so quickly?"

"No, it is just that I don't believe he wishes to be here, sir."

The dark eyebrows rose. "What has that to do with the matter?"

"But he's not a...a slave." The word was difficult to speak.

"He understands what you clearly do not. The needs of the high families must come first."

"The country's prosperity," she repeated an early lesson. "Yes, all right. But if he wants to leave, I wish to allow him to go."

"No."

She crossed her arms over her chest.

Andras tilted his head and frowned consideringly. Only a peacock's bizarre shriek broke the long silence.

Andras smiled, a tight thin expression of barely contained anger. "Either you will use Gilrohan for this purpose or I suppose... Yes. I can assign Wilde to aid you."

She was about to ask him whom he meant, when the fat steward standing near her grew very still. His eyebrows rose the fraction of an inch and he reddened.

Andras laughed. "Ah, hardly a strong response, but I know Wilde from years of association. He does not like the idea."

"My lord," the man murmured, pleading.

He ignored the steward and stared into her eyes. "Lord Gilrohan or my steward. You decide."

"Neither. You," she said flatly, though at the moment she would rather bed poor Wilde than the odious Andras.

"I am not one of the two options." He loped back up the stairs. "I suggest you take your time to think it over. This is a very serious matter and I shan't change my mind. You do not want to cross me on the subject, Lady Tabica." He sat in the carved chair and picked up the papers again. "Wilde, walk her back to her chambers. Maybe she has a few questions for you."

Wilde bowed and, without looking at Tabica, hurried to the door to open it for her.

He bowed so deeply as she passed, she could not see his face.

In the hall, she asked. "Is he serious? Could he force you to, ah, serve me?"

"Lord Andras does not indulge in frivolous threats, my lady," the steward replied after a long uncomfortable silence.

"So you'd—"

"Yes, my lady. Though I am... It must be an honor, that is to say..." The poor man's face went grey. To think that she'd been rather scared of the formidable steward. Not nearly as frightened of him as he was of her, apparently. He gave a cough and went on. "My heart, you see, my lady. It is not as strong as it once was. I-I have heard stories—"

"No, don't worry. I'll find a solution."

"Please, my lady, I beg of you. Do not think that I would not endeavor to give satisfaction, my lady. It is my life's work to serve the high—"

"Yes, yes," she interrupted again. "Please go back to your duties. I can find my chamber. "

He recovered most of his customary dignity. With his head high and his hands clasped behind his back, he took off back in the direction of the audience chamber, walking only slightly faster than usual.

Despite the fine clothes the steward wore, he was as much a slave as she'd been. For that matter, Gilrohan was one as well. And if Andras thought she'd accept that fate for again for herself... She would find a way to escape.

He'd made clear the role of the ereshkigal in the world. Called advisors to royalty, they merely manipulated whichever royal family fell to their use. The five families employed fear and occasionally the Arts to keep their chosen puppets in line.

Andras had also made clear that if one ereshkigal should rise up against another, the families would withdraw immediately and allow only the two to face each other alone. "Too many lives have been lost and the honor of the families drained away. The threat of a duel was the only way to keep the existing most powerful ones in check. D'you see? Those fights are bad enough."

She'd read an account of the yellow miasma that lay over the land that had witnessed a rare clash between ereshkigal. Strange effect.

A duel with Andras. Could she possibly survive such a thing? Why yes, if the confrontation took place in a bed. Or perhaps if she had sufficient control of her power.

She paused outside her door. Damn. She would have to say the words no one wishes to speak. With a deep breath, she pushed open the door and got it out of the way. "You were right and I was wrong."

Her voice rang out in silence. She looked around the room. Empty, except for furniture and the tree. Had he strolled out of the palace and gone on his way? Just as the pang of regret struck her, the leaves rustled and Gilrohan dropped to the floor.

He dusted the front of his tunic. "I haven't climbed a tree since the time my tutor found me hanging upside down outside his window. Must have been eight then."

She resisted the urge to fish the leaf from his hair. "You were right about Master Andras, but I will find a way to train myself. After all, others must have done it before me."

"Nope. I did some research about ereshkigals—"

"When?" Her heart gave a flutter almost like excitement—he'd thought about her while they were apart.

He brushed his hands through his hair and found the leaf on his own. He twirled it deftly between long fingers. Those fingers... "The king's record keepers are excellent. Far as I can tell, you're the first ereshkigal on record to miss childhood training."

"Oh."

How'd he get so close to her without her notice? He must still possess some wildcat traits.

"Did he offer alternatives to you?"

She shrugged.

"He didn't, I see. Or not any you cared for. It may interest you to know that I thought over the matter after you stormed out of here and I have decided that I am not afraid. No, I lie. I've decided I'm afraid you would insist I leave. I resent being ordered to service you, but I would resent it far more if another came to your bed. Or if I missed a chance to see your enchanting body and touch it again."

She could taste his scent, leather and wood smoke. The dizzying delicious taste of Gilrohan, but she must try again to convince him to stay safe. "It is the magic, I mean the Arts, in my body ensnaring you."

"Just your body, no other Arts needed. Your smile and your kisses have caught me."

Ha—and he managed to capture her with just his words.

She swallowed, hard. "We will go slow. The master Andras said to and I wouldn't let him. He might have been right."

He nodded. "You will listen to me then? If I tell you to slow down?" Just a hair closer and they'd be touching. His breath washed over her. He flashed an evil grin. "I sat in the tree and thought of you. A lovely way to spend time, by the by. I have a plan."

"You do?"

"Mmm." His eyes darkened. "I will use the skills I learned. I will tease you, bring you close to the moment. Over and over. You will learn to gain pleasure from every touch. Not just between your legs." He raised his hand. "Here." His thumb lightly touched her throat at the point of her quickening pulse "Here." A finger brushed shoulder. "Here." And then a breast. "And most of all, here." His lips skimmed her temple, a touch that sent a shiver down her back.

"Yes," she whispered. "I understand."

"Take off your dress and lie on the bed."

She hesitated.

"Ah, now, my lady, you said you would listen to me. I hesitate to say 'obey' to an ereshkigal, but—"

She deftly untied the side ribbons on the velvet gown and drew it over her head. "Don't worry about saying anything except 'my lady'. I might blast you for that." Folding the dress, she considered other ways to keep him from harm. "We need a word for safety. If you feel my power is too strong."

He raised his brows. "I will die a deliriously happy man."

"No, I mean it. Pick a word to keep you safe. I will-will find a way to hear it even in my most power-saturated state."

He frowned. "It must be a word that can reach you then."

She smiled remembering. "Fesslerat is good."

"Good. Now get onto the bed. "

She sat on the edge, untied the garters and rolled off fine knit stockings. She could feel his avid watching eyes. "You are not doing a good job of listening I said just the gown." He pointed at the bed. "Now lie down."

She rolled onto her back, still dressed in the light chemise. "Why should I wear this thing?"

He rubbed the feather-light garment between two fingers. "It might help blunt the edge. The cloth is silk. As I expected. You are growing used to your life here?"

"It sometimes feels as if I have never lived another sort of life. Other times I wake and wonder where I am and what has happened to my straw mattress.

"Makes sense," he said. "I remember the time of awakening. I felt as if I had a fever, some days seemed to drag years, and I think I skipped others altogether."

He touched her arm. A quick draw of the fingertips over her skin and she felt the tingle through her entire body.

"Good. Well." He moistened his lips, suddenly less assured. "Your master started with the, ah, core of your problem, I suppose?"

"Yes. "

"I am far weaker than he is. I will begin far away. "He untied his shirt as he spoke, pulled it off and tossed it onto the large chair. Bare-chested, he returned to the bed and eyed her. Then he leaned over her feet and kissed her instep—warm lips, the brush of his beard against her tender skin. He smiled and seemed to regain his self-confidence.

"I will start with your toes perhaps. Delicious little nibbles. And the firm flesh of your soles." He settled on the edge of the bed and lifted her foot gently onto his lap. With his back to her as if he ignored the rest of her body, he rubbed each foot—vigorous, fast rubs and then slow, gentle touches. Those almost tickled, or would have if her body hadn't already vaulted into the burn of arousal. He kissed each toe, long and luxurious tastes, flicking his tongue to the sensitive, rarely touched area between each toe.

"You have wonderful feet. And ankles." He twisted as he moved to her ankles. "Such good strong calves." His breathy voice grew thick. "God, it's too close. Too close."

She tried to pull her feet from his lap.

"No, don't concern yourself with me. You concentrate on your power. I can do this."

He stood and backed away from her. After groping for a cloth, he dipped it in cold water he rubbed it over his face and then arms. Even that seemed to arouse him. His head went back and his mouth fell open as it did when he came close to those final spasms of pleasure. The erection pushing at his trousers looked painful.

For a brief time, he resumed his touch on her body, but very soon his hands trembled and his breath turned to pants.

"Perhaps you should let yourself feel the pleasure?" she asked as he bounded away from her again.

"No...you." His sharp voice came from behind the cold cloth. "We must help you. Not me."

She sat up. "I should like it. Let me help you. Unless you don't think..."

Before he had a chance to protest, she moved from the bed and kneeled before him.

"No." But even as his spoke his hands tangled in her hair.

Gil knew that Tabica was right. The tension must end or his sanity might crack. She loosened his trousers and even that light touch threatened to send him rocketing over the edge. Hunger licked him, and then she did. The tongue daintily tasted his cock, made his legs grow weak He leaned against the trunk of the tree to keep from falling over. Her lush lips opened and she enveloped his cock with her hot, tight mouth. Deep into her mouth.

She sucked and moved on him like a woman possessed, not like the reluctant slave. Hardly mattered to his deliriously happy cock enveloped in her hot mouth but his heart lifted at the sight of her aroused and delighted. Oh it would not take more. She stroked his balls and he knew he was close. Her tongue teased the underside of his cock's head.

The exquisite convulsions hit him suddenly and hard, twisting him inside and out. He tried to pull away from her, but she kept her mouth on him, sucking and licking until the pulses died away.

"Mmm," she said, swiping the back of her hand over her swollen mouth that was glazed with what she'd taken from him. He found the sight entirely arousing. Again? Though honestly, her power over his body should not have astonished him. Now at least he might not pass out with desire.

He allowed himself a glorious moment of reveling in his weak-kneed relief but not long. He had an assignment. No lounging about.

"Now we will attend to our important business."

She backed away and lay across the bed. With a sigh of contentment, he got to back to work.

Tabica lay on her back, reassured by his lazy smile. But when he touched her, she felt his energy had been renewed, not diminished.

The eyelids, the mouth, back of the ear, each part he stroked or tongued. Until she whimpered and writhed under his touch. Her body crackled with need. A tinderbox. Never had she known the back of her knees could contain such melting longing. Sometimes he just ran his fingertips over the fine hairs on her skin, sometimes a firm, strong grip that came close to pain.

He rubbed her spine, stroking her as if she were dough. And when she would grow weak, a sharp tweak on her shoulder pulled her back. It was as if he'd done this before. Certainly as if he knew the meaning of her speechless moans and her helpless shudders.

He spoke occasionally, murmuring words of encouragement to her, more often cursing quietly under his breath and drawing away.

"You-you want me again?" she whispered.

"More than I want my next breath," he mumbled, his mouth busy on her breast.

When he flicked his tongue over her tingling nipple, she wrapped her legs around his torso. She knew that rubbing her core on his skin would drive his control to the brink, but she could not bear another moment without him filling her. She tried to urge him into her, but he pulled away and lay on his back.

"I think. Yes. You must be in control. You ride me." He arched up as she put a leg over him, but then dropped to the bed. "You...control. Don't battle against me, don't fight your skills. Let them go."

"You might be in danger." Even as she positioned herself over him, knees on either side of his hips, she had to say it again. "Being inside me." She felt the iron heat of his cock nudging urgently at her. "Not safe."

"It isn't." He gasped his agreement as she took his stiff cock in her hand. "It's so wonderful, it can't possibly be safe."

Tabica could no longer speak. She gripped his penis and moved its head over her nether lips, savoring him at her entrance—but she wanted more. Now. She positioned him and slowly, slowly slid onto the delicious thickness until he was buried all the way inside her. Almost too large—they hadn't done this in such a long time. She carefully rose and then lowered herself again, moving in a steady rhythm. Rising, falling. The diamond hard cock piercing her, she pushed down until she felt him pressed high inside her. As the tension built, her cadence broke wild. She bucked and writhed as she rode him, bracing her hands on his shoulders.

"Yes. Go," he whispered. "If-if you are ready...." He groaned.

Her body took control.

For a moment, he must have lost his restraint too, for he clutched her hips and sharply pushed high into her— but then forced himself to sink down to the bed. "No. You. No." He kept his hands on her hips. With obvious effort, he kept his body still, allowing her to thrash and move on him. With a groan close to pain, he trembled and squeezed his eyes shut.

"Wait. You must look at me," she commanded. "In my eyes. Now."

She stopped fighting, stopped struggling to impose her will onto the raging fever.

Allow it to happen, he'd told her.

Staring into the blue gold and silver of his irises kept her from spinning away, but otherwise... She bit back the urge to struggle.

In the eyes, she read him. Strength tamped back years ago and released. Now. Tenderness hidden from a society that rated it nonsense. Pain and love. Love that could fill her and keep her strong enough to release it all.

She almost heard him say the words. *I will catch you should you fall.*

She let go and dropped. Her body took control. *Let it win.* A flower unfolding, growing, shedding petals, exploding into seed. The power surged out and settled into her blood, perhaps, the way it thrummed continuously through her now and out to every bit of her body. Love? she thought as she pitched dizzily into her own heat.

For even as her limbs and heartbeat resettled the power, his hands on her hips suddenly tightened. He pulled her up and off. Her whimper of protest turned into a moan when he rolled her over and covered her with his body. With a growl, he pushed into her, all urgency and heat now. Her body's ripples of pleasure returned at once. Even as she gave the loud howl of warning, he pressed harder and his own harsh cry joined hers.

He roared her name and plunged into her again and again.

The end of her pleasure...Ah that was as lovely as always. Exquisite and pure greedy hunger exploding and transforming with each pulse into satisfaction. Delicious. The reverberating pleasure shuddered through them.

A groggy thought hit her that perhaps she must push away from their explosion to keep him safe. But the shudders of ecstasy faded into small pulses then twinges.

The storm passed. Every bone in her body melted then reformed.

He lay half on her, his eyes closed. Almost but not quite too much of his breathing weight, nearly perfect.

She swallowed, tried to speak. Swallowed again and turned to her head to look at his face near hers. "Gilrohan?"

The corners of his mouth twitched slightly.

"You're not...not injured?"

He didn't open his eyes or speak, but ever so gently he shook his head.

"Can you speak?"

"I expect so," he whispered gruffly. "But I don't know why I'd bother." The smile grew. He pulled out of her and rolled onto his side. With a groan, he hauled himself onto one elbow. "Ah, wait. I know why. To tell you I saw paradise just now." He brushed the edge of his thumb along her face. "And I felt it here." One large hand squeezed her hip. "As soon as I am able to move again, I plan on exploring you some more."

"You don't need to," she said quietly.

"Ha! So we are successful?"

"I think so. I feel as if someone has come and wiped away a thickness inside me." She stretched long and luxurious like a cat. "Turned it into shimmering dust and blew on it until it flew off."

"So you mean we don't need to do this again. Hmm. But what if I want to?"

She shifted onto her side to face him—and saw nothing but fondness. Did he mask himself? Or had she imagined love? She swallowed regret and counted herself lucky for having as much as a friend and lust. "I would be more than willing. Pure enjoyment as when we met."

For some reason, her words drove the lazy bliss from his eyes. He sighed and dragged himself up to sit cross-legged. "I forgot what you are for a moment."

"I'm Tabica. That is *who* I am."

"Daughter of Samanth. A powerful ereshkigal in your own right."

"Tchah. And you're the man who managed to shift power that defeated me. And Lord Andras."

All traces of his smile vanished completely. "Ah, Tabica, I will miss you."

"Stay with me," she coaxed.

He gently lifted her hand and kissed her knuckles. A formal gesture, not loving. "I serve my king. But I am not formed to be nothing more than a servant. Do you see?" He did not sound angry, only sad.

"Be my..." She knew the words would be dangerous but she only hesitated a moment. "Be my love."

The bleak look in the blue eyes softened but did not vanish. "I am honored," he said quietly. "But I must be on my way."

"Why?"

He turned away from her searching gaze and climbed from the bed. "You are ereshkigal. Perhaps first ranking members of the high families can approach you in friendship, but otherwise you can have nothing but servants."

For a moment, her heart grew hot with pain. He valued his dignity more than her love? But then she understood and she could not fault him for avoiding the same life she'd run away from.

"Bah," she said. "This being an ereshkigal is a nuisance."

"You seem already used to giving orders and wearing lovely clothes." He touched her chemise. "Your life has some compensations. Recall where I found you."

"I miss my home," she said at last. "More than I expected."

He opened his mouth to protest but she waved a hand at him. "Oh, not my life, not once I was declared a slave. You're right about that. But the country. Did you look around when you were there? No, I didn't think so. The hills are lovely. The trees. I never did learn their names. My mother was going to teach me. And I wonder what has happened to the people I know? What will happen now that Lerae is gone? Who's master there?"

"Ah, that I can answer. I now possess that estate."

"What?" She squealed and sat upright. "You? Why?"

"It was handed over to me several days ago as a reward for my service to the high families."

"Finding me?"

"Yes and for the inconvenience I suffered as a prisoner."

"Why aren't you there? It's nearly harvest time."

Gilrohan smiled. Once again he had to resist the urge to pull her up and into a kiss. "I am here with you."

"Who is overseeing the harvest? I swear the lord is of some use at that time and—"

"I have agents on all of my estates."

Her frown deepened. Damn, she looked adorable, all flushed, naked and filled with concern for the world she'd left behind. "But who did you leave in Lerae's place?"

"That sister of his. Adama. She's assumed the outward control, and I will make sure my agent keeps a sharp watch so she doesn't try to poison anyone again. I will do my rounds in the spring—and bring my own food."

He reflected that the ritual of the visits was his favorite task, riding through the woods and fields of his holdings. No need for entertaining the bored king or the bored court. No need to try to guess which direction the winds of intrigues blew. Just the real wind and his grumbling valet to keep him company. No need to be a sycophant.

"You have more than one estate?" She sounded flabbergasted.

"You will, too, Tabica. Vaster and far more impressive than my four small domains."

"You do enjoy telling how my life has changed," she murmured. "Or maybe you're reminding me I still carry the outlook of a peasant in my heart. Sallos knows, Andras reminds me often enough. The blister."

He laughed. That certainly must be the first time Lord Andras had been called a blister.

Tendrils of her hair, thoroughly tangled from their passionate night, lay across her face. She swiped at them impatiently. "You're cheerful. Why are you laughing?"

Cheerful did not describe how he felt, but he didn't contradict her. "I pray you never lose that outlook in your heart." He rose to his feet.

Another lock of hair brushed her cheek. Without taking her eyes off him, she raised her arms and unceremoniously gathered up her hair to weave it into a loose braid. "Are you mocking me?"

"Always. Of course. But that doesn't mean I'm lying. Your heart makes you entirely an original."

She scowled.

"Fresh to me, then. Your heart is..." He didn't say perfect, instead shrugged and allowed the sentence to die away.

She let go of her haphazard braid and went to him. Her pale body gleamed in the dying firelight. Beautiful and unashamed of her nakedness. "Hold me." Biting her lip, she added, "Please. As a friend. I know you are my friend no matter what anyone else says."

"Yes. I am."

Had they ever embraced standing? He wrapped his arms around her, marveling at how her body pressed to his brought him a surge of comfort. She twisted closer and the comfort at once grew entwined with heated interest. Confounded Sallos, perhaps they had not cured her, for his response seemed too strong after such a long night.

A pounding at the door made them jump but he tightened his arms and kissed the top of her head.

A voice outside the door called, "My lord Andras wishes to inform you he will be entering this chamber in a very short while."

He squinted at the grey pink dawn showing through the chink of the tall window's thick, burgundy coverings. They had spent the whole of the night? It had seemed such as short time as they coaxed the power from her womb.

He gathered his clothing.

She asked, "Do you want my help dressing?"

He smiled. "No, thank you. After my sojourn in Lerae's domain, I understood how absurd I must have seemed to you. I regularly don my own clothing now, much to the disgust of my valet."

"You cared what I thought of you?"

He nodded but did not look her in the face. He suspected she had the ereshkigal's skill of reading hearts when the eyes met. As they'd made love with their gazes locked, he had almost felt her plunging into his soul almost as deeply as he had plunged into her body.

He studied her round and wonderful rear end as she picked up her gown. Last time he'd see that lovely sight—but he would not give over to maudlin reflections. Plenty of leisure for that when he went on another drinking spree with his comrades, other bored young gentlemen at court.

He shook out his clothes and awkwardly scrambled into them. Why not take her offer? The life of unearned leisure would not be so different from the one he would return to.

With a sudden lurch of his heart, he realized he would not return to that old life at court. He'd serve his king of course, yet he must do more than drink with clever men, bed clever women, entertain his king by taking on amusing animal forms or the occasional more interesting task. The existence he'd enjoyed had grown empty. Blasted Savnack, this would make life more difficult. And exactly what else could a frivolous man do with himself?

Dressed in dark well-pressed trousers and tunic, Andras swept into the chamber. Despite the fact that he wasn't wearing the long robes of an ereshkigal, he made an impressive entrance. Years of practice, most likely.

His dark eyes examined Gil. "You look well."

Gil nodded. "Yes, my lord."

"How do you feel?"

He didn't ask with any personal concern in mind, naturally. Gilrohan resisted answering "beautifully fucked" and thought for a moment. "As if I'd been translated, my lord."

Andras glowered, clearly certain Gilrohan mocked him. "Hey? What does that mean?"

Gilrohan looked at Tabica as he slowly replied. "As if I had been in the wrong language and was translated at last into a sweeter far more expressive tongue."

Andras snorted and padded over to Tabica. The expensive boots he wore made no sound. A panther, dark as midnight, couldn't have moved more silently.

Perhaps Andras had morphing skills, a common enough skill among members of the high families. So common that even Gil, several generations removed, with only a trace of high family blood, still carried the crudest form. Of course he had to wait for the flow and ebb of outside forces. An ereshkigal would not be so limited.

Gil stifled protest when Andras's fingers went straight to Tabica's lower belly. His hand didn't linger long however. He pulled back as if he'd been burned.

"Ah," he breathed. "The stream is nearly unimpeded. You have a healthy pulse of power and lust, but they are not as entangled."

He gave Gil a benign smile. Ha. The panther would probably be a safer companion.

"After you have broken your fast, assuming you are well enough to travel, you may go."

Tabica started. "But perhaps he might stay. Rest a while. Sir. I mean—"

"You were all for him leaving at once last night. Now he may." He crossed his arms over his chest. "We are grateful for your service and will be sure to mention it to the king."

"But he didn't sleep all night..." Her face reddened and Gil had to smother a smile. No doubt the implications embarrassed her.

"He may rest then. And leave in a few hours." Gil, the effective tool, had done his job and was now forgotten. Lord Andras turned his full attention to Tabica. The sleek smile still touched his mouth. "Lady Tabica, we have to catch up. We have been too impeded by your problem to do proper training. For now we will clean up the messes here created by your condition and get to work at once, after that. "

The large silent steward appeared at Gil's elbow.

"Wilde will show you to breakfast and will help you ready yourself for your journey."

"But Lord Andras—" Tabica began.

"Thank you, my lord," Gil said flatly to Andras. No point in drawing this out. Gilrohan knew he would not allowed to say a proper goodbye to her or even bow over her hand where he might administer a chaste kiss.

֎

He rode back to Marchosia, Lord Andras's hungry smile haunting him. As he traveled, he decided to visit his estates right away instead of waiting until spring. In particular, he would go to his newest property, the one in the northland that had once belonged to the minor baron, Lord Lerae.

And by all the demons, he'd find a way to see Lady Tabica again.

Chapter Eight

Thrown into work, Tabica's mind reeled from thinking and reading, her body ached from controlling the strange powers soaring through it. The roar of sheer mindless need had at last been muffled. Not silenced though. During the day, she had no room to think of anything other than the work. But many nights, she lay awake and wondered how he could have walked away so easily. Her vivid dreams of Gilrohan left her wet and often jangling close to the edge of release.

She knew the patina of those dreams lingered when she went to her lessons. Tabica didn't speak of the dreams, but Andras's shining dark eyes missed nothing. His hand might rest for a moment on the back of her head those mornings, or he might brush her arm. No provocative motions, but enough to show he knew. Her body, roused again, remembered their peculiar fiery mating that had been more of a battle than love-making.

His manner changed, became less formal. She suspected he intended more encounters with her to test his powers against hers. The images conjured the same odd, nauseated excitement. An abnormally patient man,

Andras must have been waiting for some signal. She would give none. The twisting of her body in his arctic presence chilled her. She craved heat and even laughter. Frivolity.

She stumbled into lessons after breakfast one morning, filled with the night's yearning. Even more elegantly garbed than usual, Andras showed his disapproval of her gown with a raised brow and looking her up and down. "You're not ready."

Tabica glanced down at her fine silk overdress with lace that allowed glimpses of the flesh of her arms and legs. Did he consider it too daring? "Ready for what?"

"You are attending the guild hall with me this morning. Clearly we must work on your non-verbal skills. But I suspected that already." He erased his small leer before he turned to the steward. "Hurry. She'll require help."

The steward bowed and rushed to summon Tabica's two maids.

Tabica returned to her chambers, fear churning her stomach. The huge gold and snow building had loomed in her future since she'd spotted it on that first ride through Marchosia. Ugh. She did not know why a building that was not a prison could cause such fear.

Ah, but perhaps it was a prison. Waiting to jerk away her freedom. Nerves, she supposed. Not enough sleep and nerves made her imagination grow dark.

She allowed the maids to remove her clothes—hard to get used to being so passive. A thick black under-gown clung to her and then the heavy ornate overgown threatened to suffocate her. The scarlet gown sparkled with gems forming patterns of the beasts of the ereshkigals. The black ereshkigal robes last, the scarlet stripes matching the ceremonial gown, the touches of ermine tickling rather than soothing her neck. She would drown in the layers of clothing. Straight shoulders, slow walk, chin up. She felt ridiculous, but one of her maids, a silent woman who never offered an opinion did so now. "You are lovely, my lady. A vision."

For the journey into Marchosia, they had an entourage of five carriages and four outriders.

"Why so much bother?" she asked as she settled in the plush velvet interior of the carriage. "An ereshkigal doesn't need protection."

Andras tapped his fingers on his knee. "Appearances. Don't you understand that by now? One's outward show means almost as much as reality in our world."

"Your world."

"Our world."

"Yours."

"Ours, Tabica."

Just like the arguments she used to have with Yeva when they were little girls. Whichever of them could repeat the word often enough would win the battle. She looked out the window and grinned.

"You're not a little girl any longer," Andras said.

She made a rude sound. "I wish you'd stop reading my thoughts. It's rude."

Suddenly, Andras lurched from his seat and grabbed her wrists. For the first time since they'd been in her bed, he seemed on the verge of losing control.

"You underestimate everything." His quiet but harsh voice scared her more than any scream. "Your power, your ability to cause devastation. Yourself. I must use whatever I can to make you ereshkigal. To make you part of...this. Do you understand? It is important."

His fingers on her wrists hurt, but she didn't speak. Instead she stared into his eyes. Very well. If he would read her thoughts she would do the same.

Hot desire. Anger. Cat's eyes. And something else. An animal pacing its cage. Or a small boy in a closet? She blinked. The images vanished. And he sat back in his seat, breathing hard.

Neither of them spoke again. For the first time since they'd met, he avoided her gaze. He pretended to stare out the window. As the carriage slowed to wind its way through the streets of the city, he spoke at last, dry as always. "Remind me to explain how to read surface rather than deeper thoughts. Your strength makes you crude."

Relieved that he'd returned to his usual manner, she pressed her hands together in the acceptable ereshkigal resting posture. "I will try harder."

He made a sound that could have been agreement or derision. She didn't care, for the building loomed now, even larger than her memory. Oh if only she hadn't eaten such a large breakfast.

She closed her eyes.

"You will do well," he said unexpectedly. "You have come far in your lessons. Just remain quiet and all will go smoothly. Do not, I beg of you, say 'bah'."

Tabica smiled.

That was the last moment she felt like smiling for several hours. She was ushered into a small room where perhaps thirty people waited. Not so dreadful, she supposed, but then the crowd formed around her and she was marched into another far larger chamber. Murmuring voices echoed through the room as large as a wheat field—with a ceiling miles high. And jammed front to back with people.

Her heart jammed somewhere near her tonsils. The thousands of faces turned to her, fell silent and stared.

And waited.

Lord Andras appeared at her side. Had he used some trick to impress the crowd? She supposed so, but now she had to concentrate, listen to his words and try to calm the horrendous thumping of her heart.

His sonorous voice rose, chanting long passages of a particularly boring book she was supposed to have studied. At the end of his long recital, they made their sedate way through the bowing crowd to where the king stood.

"What's he doing here?"

"This is your induction to your proper place. Of course he'd attend."

"Induction to the gild? Why didn't you tell me?" she whispered.

"I informed you days ago that you would be coming to Marchosia."

She recalled the passing mention of Marchosia one evening. "But this?" she began.

"Enough. You are overreacting. Why else would you reenter the city?"

For the sake of entertainment? But then she recalled that Lord Andras did not believe in amusement.

Panic soon gave way to boredom. After the tedious ceremony, petitioners came forward one by one, and she half listened to their complaints, half wondered when she would be allowed to escape.

She woke from her thoughts when Andras's voice grew impatient. He held out his hand as if he were a healer—or he was trying to stop the words of the messenger.

"The ereshkigal do not travel. No."

She perked up. Travel? What a wonderful idea.

"But it is necessary in this case, my lord." The flustered messenger looked at her, pleading. She blinked and wondered why he seemed familiar. The messenger addressed Andras but watched her. "Ah. We have found no precedents. There seems to be some problems."

Her breath caught when she understood where she'd seen him before. He was from Lord Lerae's manor. Nollmet, one of the lord's advisors.

Andras prompted impatiently, "What sort of problems?"

"Odd residues of magic—of the Arts," Nollmet amended. "We have had no knowledge of or official training for the...Arts for many years and with practitioners who have not always been aware—" His face reddened.

"Explain."

He gave a small cough and pulled a piece of parchment from his sleeve. "Three inexplicable cases of cows walking on their hind legs. At least three women in their fifties giving birth. A bird that speaks plainly hopping around the woods and spooking farmers."

Andras mumbled something under his breath about idiocy.

The messenger continued, more nervous. "A dog that gave birth to a litter of cats. Another dog that is now a bitch. As well as a rooster who is now laying eggs. One woman whose voice has gone quite low and claims that she has grown a ..."

Nollmet took a deep breath, glanced at Tabica and finished. "And various other unusual occurrences, my lord.

"Enough. This nonsense doesn't require an ereshkigal. A simple practioner."

"My lord, the woman who has turned into a man was Belza, a practitioner once removed from the high family of Worth." The messenger cleared his throat. "My master has done some research here in Marchosia and has discovered there has never been a case such as this in living history.

"Your master said you should approach us. And your master is Lord Gilrohan."

"Yes," Nollmet admitted.

The name seemed to shoot through Tabica's heart and she knew Andras watched her. He had taught her well and she knew her face betrayed nothing. And she was not so stupid as to catch his eye.

A low murmur rose from the audience as they waited for another word from Andras. No one dared speak in a normal voice, but she supposed they all knew better than to expect him to reach any speedy decisions. He did not believe in rushing his words or choices. Usually.

"Yes," he said with sudden fierceness. The side of her face prickled, but she would not meet that concentrated stare.

He at last swiveled to face the representative from the northland. "We will travel there within seven days."

CRSO

Gilrohan went out to meet Nollmet and his guard who arrived exhausted but bringing word from Marchosia. The long ignored northlands were to be visited by not just one but two ereshkigals.

"They come soon, my lord."

Gilrohan didn't know if this was the worst idea he'd cooked up in a long life of stupid notions. Andras had said it. Clean up the messes she made. It would bring her to him again.

She'd see that he'd done what he could to improve her old home. He'd never bothered to interfere in his estates' workings before and he learned he rather liked making improvements and seeing the effects. The gold and jewels he'd discovered in Lerae's bedroom proved enough to purchase some decent furnishings for the manor. True, he suspected the wealth came from previous ransoms but he reasoned that he'd earned it by stopping the northland baron from taking any more prisoners.

CRSO

The ereshkigals arrived in a stately caravan.

Tabica gracefully stepped from the carriage, accepted the steward's help rather than jumping down. Would she have jumped down before he'd found her?

Gilrohan's insides swooped at her appearance. More than sexual excitement, though the tingling filled him.

She seemed taller, perhaps only because she held her shoulders straighter and her head higher. The clouds of wild hair now lay in complicated braids styled as any Marchosian lady with a properly trained army of maids. Her smile had been tamed as well, he saw with a sinking heart. For a moment, he wished he hadn't discovered her,

188

that she still possessed the raw, unpolished air, the bare feet, but that was sentimental idiocy.

He bowed to them both, deep and formal. "You honor the northlands."

"You know perfectly well why we're here. I'm only allowing this because I want Lady Tabica to rid herself of this absurd longing for her home and you."

Judging from Tabica's indignant squawk of "what?", he'd managed to keep this secret from her.

Andras looked impatient. "Yes, do you actually suppose dancing cows would be worthy of an ereshkigal's notice? Perhaps I have rushed your induction, my lady. But I have reasons. Including this man who has been useful but can hardly be worthy of more notice."

"Worthy. You are fond of that word, Lord Andras," she said, scorn in her voice.

Andras merely looked amused, like an indulgent parent. "And you are fond of inappropriate outbursts. Please keep your voice low."

They walked into the familiar keep, which immediately struck Tabica as small and shabby. The receiving chamber, that had once seemed the most elegant spot possible, had been cleaned more thoroughly than she had ever seen any room in the keep scrubbed, fabrics replaced and yet still seemed cramped and tattered after her time in the world of an ereshkigal.

She craned her neck looking for familiar faces. For a moment, she felt indignant that he would replace all of the people she'd known but then recalled that they weren't beloved faces—just familiar.

The only beloved face was the one watching her now. He looked too pale and drawn.

"Have you been ill?" she asked in a low voice while Andras gave orders to Wilde.

"I have recently attempted a morph. Merely for the practice of it." Gilrohan grinned. It wasn't fair that one smile could make her dizzy.

Perhaps she showed her response too clearly, for he fell silent until Andras turned to them. Gil bowed and ushered them into the main receiving chamber and offered them seats.

Tabica accepted a chalice of weak wine and turned her attention back to Gil. "Have your skills expanded?"

"I have discovered that I am now able to retrieve myself from morphs, my lady. Feel like I've been attacked and beaten afterwards but it is interesting."

"I thought so. I must have awakened your skills, as you did mine," she said slowly and looked at Andras for confirmation.

Bored, he nodded. But she knew better than to trust that blasé exterior. He thought the subject fascinating.

"Yes, your skills are proving more interesting than I had suspected," he grudgingly admitted to Gilrohan. "So tell me of your peculiar animals." He inspected the bowl of fruits and selected several grapes. "Not your morphs, the abnormal loose powers floating about the place."

Gilrohan again recited a list of strange occurrences. "The local folk assure me that such things had never happened before, my lord."

"They are a superstitious lot here in the northlands." The ereshkigal ate a grape before continuing with his usual follow up to that. "Hardly witnesses that I would trust."

"Bah." Tabica shoved back the chair, impatient with Andras and Gilrohan's on again off again formal manner.

She had already asked Andras why they had traveled seven long days to the manor if he didn't believe the reports. He hadn't given a straight answer before and that outburst about ridding her of her passions struck her as ridiculous. All this way for emotional nonsense? Andras had no time or patience for anything resembling a personal life. He would not squander so many days on her private concerns.

Restless, she wandered the perimeter of the room, staring out the small windows. At least the green velvet hills stretched vast and colorful as she'd recalled. Everything else had changed. Or perhaps she had.

Gilrohan remained tall and splendid. She allowed herself the pleasure of studying him again. "What have you done with Lady Adama?"

He deftly peeled an apple and handed her a slice on a linen napkin. "I think that Adama and her fat husband must have understood my frequent references to poisoning, my lady. As soon as they could, they bustled off. Something about not being able to put off a long-promised visit to another manor. I expect they will return the moment they hear I'm gone."

She grinned and wished she could have witnessed the exchanges with Lerae's sister. Not as terrible as her brother, Adama could have her moments of cruelty nevertheless. No doubt Gilrohan's superior air and knowledge of "magic" would have scared the woman into fits.

Smiling at Gilrohan was a mistake. Andras, who'd been in a bear of a mood for days, rose to his feet and snapped, "Show us to our quarters."

Gilrohan bowed and summoned his steward. Tabica should have known Andras meant trouble when he pulled the steward aside to speak to the trembling man rather than allow his own man Wilde to deal with the matter.

When they left Gilrohan, the steward led them to the chambers once used by Lerae.

The bed she'd once shared with Gilrohan had new hangings. Wilde hurried forward to remove Andras's traveling robe and carefully lay it across the clothespress.

"And where will I be housed?" she asked Gilrohan's steward. The poor man's mouth opened and closed but no sound came out. He looked at the trunks and she saw her own. "Oh. I see," she said. "Thank you. You may go."

Andras dismissed the stony-faced Wilde.

She waited until they were alone to turn to him. "What is going on?"

"We will be sharing these quarters."

"We will not." She put her hands on her hips and ignored the perilous light in her master's eyes. "You forget that you inducted me into the gild. That means I am a full-fledged ereshkigal. You no longer make my decisions for me. "

"Do not make me regret this journey."

"I have no responsibility for your regrets," she said. "I owe nothing to you but my gratitude, of course. You told me so yourself that first day. I paid my debt when I gave you youth again."

Andras grew pale. His dark eyes glittered dangerously. "I did not know what a burden it is."

Tabica flinched at the pain in his voice. He'd never sounded so passionate before. Her blood ran cold at his next words. "I had forgotten the ridiculous hungers and longings. You brought them back as well. You look so much like your mother. "

She backed away. "My mother? You knew her well?"

"Samanth had promised to be with me."

Holy Savnack. Her mother and Andras had almost been mates? But she didn't have time to comprehend or imagine more for he moved toward her now with slow but purposeful steps. She swallowed hard. "That couldn't be. Ereshkigal must not marry. You told me that."

"Not as my wife. But we would have been mates. I thought her dead. It was worse to learn she left me for some nothing of a man. And you will not do the same to me. No."

The scratch at the door interrupted the startling confession. She withdrew to the corner of the chamber to hide and think.

Lord Gilrohan walked into the room. He started a formal invitation to them to share a meal, but his words faltered and his eyes narrowed at the numerous trunks. *Stop it,* she wanted to shout. *You left without me. You left too easily.*

She wanted to tear at the ties holding the clothes to his body, pull him to her, throw herself into his arms, climb him, kiss him until he weakened. Without hesitation, she moved from her teacher's side and put her hand on Gil's arm. What better way to solve the problem of Andras than with a demonstration of affection? She would stop short with ripping the clothes from their bodies.

"No." Andras's voice was deceptively pleasant. "You may not. Tabica, I won't let you."

"No?" She whirled around. "I will follow my duties as ereshkigal. More than that is not your concern."

Andras looked as pained as he did when she proved slow on her lessons. "Haven't I made myself clear? You're mine."

Gilrohan heart plummeted at the remark but he quickly recovered and even wanted to cheer when he saw the dismay on Tabica's face. He gave a low whistle. "She's no longer a slave, my lord, and she belongs to no one. You understand that better than anyone else. My lord."

Tabica did not even glance at him. "Stop. I will fight my own battles."

"Oh. Naturally, my lady," Gilrohan growled. He dropped onto the bed and crossed his arms over his chest. No one made mention of his outrageous action of sitting in the company of his superiors.

They wouldn't. The two ereshkigals glowered at each other like dogs about to skirmish over a bone.

Tabica even bared her white teeth. "We settle this now, Andras. I don't know what you want from me. You did not even particularly like the-the time we did mate."

Andras laughed—the first time Gil could recall hearing that rusty sound. "You know nothing. That seared me. You turned me inside out and left me a changed man."

Blessed Sallos. The ereshkigal was human after all. Gilrohan knew exactly what he meant about Tabica in bed.

"No." Tabica turned white. Gilrohan considered barging between them, grabbing her and informing her that being turned inside out and seared was a wonderful experience and she should only do that with him from now on.

"You thought I lied when I talked about your power?" Andras spoke so quietly, Gil could barely hear. "I don't mean on the weather or the talking dogs here. I meant on me. I will have you."

"Not if she doesn't—" Gilrohan began, but a spark of something blue and crackling sent him diving for the floor. He came up with a sword in his hand. Gil wasn't ereshkigal but he wouldn't be threatened—and wouldn't allow Tabica to be, either.

"Don't bother with toys. You hold no sort of power that could harm me." Andras spared a sneer for Gilrohan.

"I hold power." Tabica grabbed her teacher's shoulder. "I am the one you should fear."

Andras transferred all of his attention to her again. "Yes, you're correct. I have lost my patience."

He reached up and captured her hand with his fingers. She did not move.

Damn, did he somehow hold her prisoner? Gilrohan took a step toward them, still gripping the sword but keeping it lowered at his side.

Eyes glittering with hunger, Andras drew her hand to his lips.

No, please no. Gilrohan had enough pride not to shout the words aloud, but they jammed in his throat.

"No, please no." Tabica twisted her hand.

Andras tightened his grip.

"Stop," Gilrohan said. Ready for the blue sparks, he jumped away as they shot near him and then leaped over the next spurt as he moved closer. "Let go of her."

Tabica shook her head without looking away from Andras. "Gilrohan, he will hurt you. Go away."

"Looks to me like he's hurting you." He stopped moving closer as a yellow mist surrounded the two figures.

The evil omen? Surely the yellow miasma was a myth, a symbol of anger.

"No, of course I wouldn't harm you, Tabica," Andras murmured. "I did not kiss you before. That was a mistake. Allow me to try again."

"Let go of me." Tabica pushed away from Andras.

The mist grew thicker. Demons, this was no myth. The room shook.

Gilrohan slipped as the floor trembled but caught himself before he hit the stones. The two figures in the mist did not appear affected by the shudders running through the room.

Andras looped an arm around her waist. Gilrohan instinctively moved closer to stop him.

Tabica swiveled in his arms and the yellow fog spread. She struck his shoulder. An eerie howling filled the air. A pitcher on the stand shattered. Gilrohan clapped hands over his ears, which might have had pokers pressing through them. Which of them created the horrendous sound? Impossible to tell.

A fire broke out on the bed, glowing orange in the thick fog. Gilrohan rushed to pull down the bed curtains and smother the flames.

The battling ereshkigals, still intent upon each other, did not appear to notice what happened around them.

"I will never again touch a man unless I choose to," Tabica shouted into Andras's face. She pulled away from her mentor's grip, and Gilrohan wanted to applaud her—until the whole mantel crumbled to the floor.

Distant wails of fear drifted through the window. The sky had turned black tinged with the evil yellow.

"Enough," he shouted over the wails and howling. He considered trying to attack Andras again, when he saw Tabica stumble. Her face took on the ghastly green hue of the sky. Gil stumbled and cursed as he circled around the room toward her, a trip that took too long. The ereshkigals had shifted space as well.

She did not move or look at him as Gil wrapped his arms around her suddenly thin form, wondering and hoping he could still lend her strength.

Wind blasted through the room, whipping speech from Gilrohan's mouth and spewing the foul yellow haze farther.

She leaned against him and he held her tight, one arm across the top of her breasts, his other hand clasping her waist. His arm pressed to the bare cold and clammy skin above her breasts.

"Stay strong," he whispered, more a prayer than instructions—he wasn't even sure she could hear him above the wailing. She trembled and then seemed to grow. Heat filled her and almost burned his arm.

Gil let go of her and opened his mouth to catch his breath in the wild air that whipped clothing and papers in frenzied circles around the room. He was exhausted and weak, like a fish landed on the ground. Considering what he must do—ha, if he were a landed fish he'd need more than the strength to flip himself back into the water—he must somehow cause the whole pond to rise up and cover him.

He saw his chance as, through the haze, he noticed Andras did not move. He certainly focused on something inside himself or perhaps Tabica. Keeping an eye out for the hot blue light, Gil careened over to him. He reached for Andras's wrist and twisted and neatly hauled up and behind the man's back. That would grab the idiot's attention at least. Treachery of course—laying hands on an ereshkigal was a death sentence, but if he did nothing, the whole keep would collapse around them. Perhaps the whole of the north country.

"Stop!" he shouted into the ereshkigal's ear. "You are going to kill us. You're destroying everything."

The wind and the terrible growls vibrating through the air ceased as suddenly as a blown-out candle. Tabica said something, but Gilrohan's hearing and sight were already shutting down.

Andras somehow untwisted. He easily yanked his hand from Gilrohan's grip and stepped back, rubbing at his wrist. "Now that is interesting," he remarked conversationally but so loud Gilrohan could hear. "You hurt me and yet you're still alive."

Searing pain hit Gilrohan's hands. The room went black as he collapsed.

Tabica screamed again. As her throat opened, the earth rumbled beneath them. She pressed her hands over her mouth to stop the destructive noise issuing from her throat. Breathing hard, she dropped to her heels to turn over the grey, still form and feel for a pulse. "What have you done to him?"

Andras squatted by Gilrohan. "Oddly enough, I have not killed him. No, Lady Tabica. Don't give me such a look. It's a protective measure that I have no control over. I suppose the pain merely took longer than usual to reach him. "

He reached for Gilrohan and Tabica shoved him hard out of the way with her shoulder. Andras straightened, but said nothing. She spared a moment to notice that the peculiar light in his eyes had died, but she hardly cared about him. She stared down at the sluggish pulse beating at Gilrohan's neck.

"Don't die, damn you." Raging, she slammed her hand against his shoulder and chest. She lurched forward and pressed her face to his throat.

Andras, calm as usual, spoke. "I admit he has some peculiar strengths. But still. You waste yourself." Soft footsteps told her he left the room, but she didn't bother to turn around.

"Live." She tore at Gil's clothing and then sat up to yank off her own more complex gown. His flesh paled every second. She flung herself onto him. Lying skin to skin on the floor, she tuned her heartbeat to his. "You're mine. Live."

CR☙

A quiet familiar voice woke Gilrohan. A woman murmured about working with the Arts. The skilled female he'd hired to set things straight. Hold on, she turned into a woman again. Of course. He'd lured out the ereshkigals and they'd done their job. Demons, he hoped they'd left the building intact as well. Stupid of him to think that he could somehow gain the upper hand with Andras, that powerful bastard.

"I'd been struggling for days," Belza continued. She had to be speaking to someone else. "The man did it with a wave a hand—well, not really—but nearly that. And all the odd effects dissipated. I've been to check. One simple motion. He's amazing."

"He's horrible." Tabica's voice nearby, perhaps next to Gil—wherever that was.

A comfortable place, at any rate. Nearly perfect with Tabica there.

Gilrohan opened his eyes. He lay on the bed in the old lord's chamber. The two women stood on either side of the bed. Belza had on the apron she'd used as a healer. Tabica wore a retiring gown, her glorious hair lay undressed and down her back.

He tried to say her name but it came out as a croak.

Tabica spun around. Her face glowed.

"Tabica." This time his thick tongue let him form the word.

Without speaking, she leaned over him and gently kissed his face, small sweet kisses from his forehead to his chin.

Ah. He'd won. His body might feel as if he'd been de-boned and he might well be under a sentence of death, but Gilrohan had won.

"Mine." He managed to lift a hand and stroke her cheek.

"Yes." Her whisper warmed his ear. "And mine." She put her hand on his chest, over his heart.

"Very touching." The bastard Andras must have his soft boots on again. How long had he been there?

Belza gave a small squeak. She leaned close and whispered, "Oh. I ah, think I will...ah. Good day, my lord. My lady. Glad you're better, Lord Gilrohan." She hurried from the room.

Belza wasn't a coward—likely Andras had aimed one of his darkest looks at her. Gilrohan hauled himself up to lean against the pillows. His unwelcome visitor leaned a hip against the desk and glowered.

"My lord." Gil wished he could speak above a rasping whisper. "Have you left my property in a shambles?"

Andras raised a dark brow. Surely he'd practiced that in a mirror. "On the contrary."

"What do you mean?"

Tabica started to answer but Andras silenced her by interrupting. "Once you made the error of touching me, the disagreement with Lady Tabica came to an end. You stopped the storm and apparently shored up Lady Tabica's strength that she unwisely turned against me. As for the so-called reasons you brought us here, as I had suspected, you exaggerated the problems." He adjusted his cuff and smoothed the edge of his ereshkigal robe. "And considering that she can't be well-trained, that healer you hired is fairly proficient. Blizzard or whatever her name is."

"I suppose I should thank you for putting things right here, my lord." Gilrohan rubbed a hand over his dry mouth. His fingers encountered the scratch of a beard on his chin and he wondered how long he'd been unconscious. "When does the execution take place?"

"Whose?"

"Mine, my lord. I'm not such a fool to think that I can get away with assaulting you."

Andras's eyes narrowed. "I am not such a fool to get into a duel with the Lady Tabica again. She informed me that you were to be spared. I do not argue the point."

Gilrohan pushed himself up higher. Blast it all, Andras feared Tabica more than he feared Gil. He considered drawing the dagger from his boot and flinging it at Andras, just to demonstrate his own teeth. Stupid plan. For one, he wasn't wearing his boots. For another, he'd best get used to her strength. Her hand over his heart moved to his shoulder. As if she could read his thoughts, she clutched him. For all he knew, she could read his thoughts. Another thing he must teach himself to accept, perhaps.

He couldn't wait to learn.

Andras sighed. "I am not a brute." He muttered something that Gil swore was "merely an idiot", but that would not be possible. Not from Lord Andras's lips.

"I need Lady Tabica." The ereskigal held up a hand. "Forgive me, do not lunge at me, you fool. I did not make myself clear. The gild needs her. The imbalance of four has not been easy and we knew a fifth had to appear eventually. She may not wish to serve but she must."

Gilrohan shot a glance at Tabica. "Why do you tell me these things, my lord? She is her own woman."

"She insists she will remain here. With you."

If Gilrohan could think of an appropriate tune, he would have burst into song. If his legs had enough strength, he would have danced her around the room. He could only fold his hand over the nape of her neck and pull her down. Soft warm lips met his. They sank into a delicious kiss.

"Excuse me. You are inappropriate and disgusting."

Gilrohan loosed his grip on her, but she didn't straighten. Instead she pulled herself onto the bed and settled close to him. She sat up, leaning against pillows and smiled down at him.

Staring into her dark eyes so she could read the truth of it, he said, "She is more than welcome to remain here. With me. I love her."

Gilrohan couldn't stop himself from glancing sideways for the bolt of blue flame to come from Andras. But the ereshkigal merely wrinkled his nose. "I would protest that a morphlange did not deserve to be paired with such a skilled woman, but I know that you have as yet undiscovered depths. By Sallos, you showed as much two days ago when you managed to interrupt our ...ah...disagreement."

"I was out that long?" Gil muttered to Tabica, who nodded.

Andras ignored the interruption. "Very few have interfered with an ereshkigal and lived to tell the story. You came between two." He pursed his lips and frowned thoughtfully. "And then there is the fact that her mother mated with the worst sort of commoner and yet managed to produce a most powerful ereshkigal."

Gil felt the tension drain from his weakened body. Good thing he didn't have to make any more fruitless attempts on Andras. "What do you want from me?"

Andras folded his arms. "I require you to explain to her that she must return to Marchosia."

Gilrohan shrugged. "She must decide what is best. But why do you think she should, my lord? You and I both know that the real business does not take place in the gild hall or at the king's court. Many of the Arts must be practiced in solitude."

"So you did pay some attention to Blongette."

"No, I paid attention at court, my lord. I had to." His heart soared. They might abandon that existence for much of the year. "My lord. How often does the whole gild meet?"

Andras wore a pained expression. "Thrice a year under normal circumstances."

Gil pulled himself up, delighted to feel he'd already gained back much of his strength. He kissed Tabica's cheek. "Could you stand trips to Marchosia three times a year, love?"

Andras made a rumbling sound, presumably a threat. "No. Marchosia is the seat of power. She must remain close."

She said, "I know the other three of our kind do not live within a day's journey to Marchosia. You told me so yourself."

"Ah, but they are not as distant as these forsaken, back of beyond northlands."

She grinned at Gil. He suspected she recalled his similar words about the barony.

"Give me the longer projects. All the more stubborn work," she said. "And send word when you need me. If we repair the roads between here and the city, the journey would be cut in half and you'd get the messengers here as often as you please."

Gil wanted to applaud. She'd obviously planned their life while he lay unconscious.

Andras scowled. "The day-to-day business and emergencies. I am growing old, and—"

Tabica laughed. "You're not old any more."

"Blast you." Andras went to a chair and sank down into it.

Gil cleared his throat. "My lord, may I point out that she is not yet socially fit for your meetings and for court?"

Rather than grow offended, Tabica understood Gil's tactic and eagerly added, "It's true. I can't hold my face blank the way you can, Andras. I'd laugh or something and drag down that splendid solemn show of power you put on."

"Bah." Andras made a very rude noise and rose from the chair. "You are both going to cause me a great deal of trouble, aren't you?" He didn't storm from the room, but came close. The door slammed behind him.

"Bah?" Tabica's mouth dropped open. "He said 'bah'? Oh dear, I've been a bad influence on him."

"You are a wonderful influence. But he can't have you." His arms must have already gained strength because Gil managed to pull her against him. "You are mine." He took advantage of her slightly parted lips to give her a full kiss on the mouth. She purred and tugged him even closer.

Author's Note

The odd names Marchosia, Savnack, Ereshkigal, etc. are from various demons through many ages and religions. Here's an interesting source for the demons' histories:

http://www.deliriumsrealm.com/delirium/mythology/demon_list.asp

Also tucked into the story are the changed names and adulterated plotline from a 1960s half-hour show.

About the Author

Summer Devon is the erotica pen name of author Kate Rothwell. To learn more about Summer Devon, please visit http://www.summerdevon.com or send an email to summerdevon@comcast.net. You can visit Summer/Kate's blog at http://katerothwell.blogspot.com

Look for these titles

Now Available

Learning Charity

How would you feel if you found out life, as you know it, is all a lie?

New Beginnings: Carpe Diem
© *2006 Tilly Greene*

After the 3rd world war, Earth is drastically damaged. By the 23rd century generations have passed, the facts twisted, history revised so it is unrecognizable and below ground a utopian society is established. Or is it?

Major Cooper Sayer, an imposing intelligent member of the special security forces, and Maris Gower, a peaceful soul who works in the New American Central Library, are an officially partnered couple. Life is comfortable, full of love for each other, and yet it took them less than fifteen minutes to decide on a radical change.

With the dangers of residing below ground growing daily and the low life expectancy rate continually dropping, chances of a long and happy life together are becoming remote. The complete trust Maris has in Cooper is never questioned, even when he tells her they are going above for a chance at a longer life. A place that she has always believed meant instant death and he knows better.

Available now in ebook from Samhain Publishing.

When two strangers meet by chance, their shared ecstasy challenges cultural differences and changes the course of their future.

Taboo
© 2006 Jordanna Kay

Two societies have lived apart on a remote planet for generations. At the top of the Dwelling live the Aerotaun, people who have built wings to help them fly. The bottom is occupied by the Marimar, hearty swimmers who live and feed by the sea. Because of the mystery surrounding their ancestors' landing, suspicions and distrust thrive between the cultures.

Until a taboo encounter occurs on an isolated beach.

Ariana, an Aerotaun, cannot resist the seductive allure of the forbidden Andreus. Their few days alone ignite sexual exploration and uninhibited ecstasy. But when Ariana finally learns the shocking secret about their purpose on the planet, she must decide if her heart belongs with her people or the sexy Marimar.

Available now in ebook from Samhain Publishing.

Enjoy the following excerpt from *Taboo*...

He was forbidden.

Ariana hovered behind the branches of a tree, where she stole glimpses of a lone man on the beach. He was a Marimar, that she was sure of. His wide chest and sculpted shoulders told the story of a man with strong lungs and powerful arms.

She had not seen one this close before. But then again, she had not ventured this far from the Dwelling either.

Ariana settled on a heavy limb and watched him hobble along the sand. He must have injured his ankle, for his gait was strange, more of a limp.

Even so, her mouth watered at the corded muscles on his legs. The small red cloth at the juncture of his legs did not cover much of his warm tawny-colored skin.

He was a surprising sight for her to see today, the first day of her solitary journey. She'd left early this morning, slipping out before Hanken could notice her gone. She must make this decision on her own, not have her betrothed's soft whispers distracting her.

The man below stumbled, then fell to his knees, his roar of pain sending birds into flight.

Without thought, Ariana dropped from the tree limb and landed on the warm sand only feet away from him.

The Marimar snapped his head up, eyes like the deep ocean waters widened in alarm. But then his face softened, the corners of his full lips curled.

"Aren't you a lovely sight."

His voice skated down her spine, setting her wings fluttering. She cleared her throat, found courage in the crossing of her arms. "My name is Ariana. Do you need assistance?"

"Ariana." He rolled the word with a sensual twist, sparking heat deep inside her belly. "I am Andreus."

She swallowed and stepped forward. Never had she been so close to a Marimar. Usually they were several hundred feet below.

"You-you are hurt."

He nodded, then with a grimace rose to his feet. Lifting one foot tenderly, he tried to hop away from the water's edge.

"I can help you." Ariana took another step closer to him, the scent of salt and something else-something wild and raw-tickled her nose.

Andreus raised a dark brow, but leaned on her shoulder. His weight and strength were far more than she ever imagined. Hanken, and others like her, were of slight build. It made them lighter and easier to fly.

She helped him hobble up the beach to a line of trees, where a make-shift shelter jutted out across the dry sand. Once inside, he dropped to the ground. "I thank you."

Ariana pulled her gaze from the hard curves of his chest, where virtually no hair covered his bronzed skin. He fascinated her. Her fingers itched to touch the long length of his legs, the broadness of his back.

"How will you make it back?"

He smiled. "I must wait for my ankle to heal. I can not swim like this, nor can I walk."

"Oh." She fiddled with her belt, jiggling the wings on her back.

"And you?" His sea-colored eyes stared into hers without reservation. "Have you been blown off-course?"

Discover eBooks!

THE FASTEST WAY TO GET THE HOTTEST NAMES

Get your favorite authors on your favorite reader, long before they're out in print! Ebooks from Samhain go wherever you go, and work with whatever you carry—Palm, PDF, Mobi, and more.

Printed in the United Kingdom
by Lightning Source UK Ltd.
121069UK00001B/328

9 781599 983967